# SWORD SONG

## THE ISLE OF DESTINY SERIES BOOK 2

## TRICIA O'MALLEY

LOVEWRITE PUBLISHING

SWORD SONG

*The Isle of Destiny Series*

*Book 2*

Copyright © 2017 by Lovewrite Publishing
All Rights Reserved

Cover Design:
Rebecca Frank Cover Designs
Editor:
Elayne Morgan

If you would like to do any of the above, please seek permission first by contacting the author at: info@triciaomalley.com

*DEDICATED TO MY FRIENDS — THE ONES WHO WILL DROP EVERYTHING TO ANSWER MY CALL, THE ONES WHO LISTEN WITHOUT JUDGMENT, THE ONES WHO ARE MY SISTERS. I LOVE YOU ALL.*

*"Always trust your gut. It knows what your head hasn't figured out yet."*

# CHAPTER 1

"Another one of you? You're getting to be quite the little pests." Sasha Flanagan swore as she circled a silver-eyed man whose unblinking stare never left her face. His body coiled like a spring as he watched her every move, waiting to pounce.

Deciding to ruffle his feathers a little, Sasha dipped forward and lashed out with a slim iron sword she'd fashioned for just such occasions. Pleased to see the silver-eyed man jump back, she pushed forward.

"I don't know where you come from or what you want with me, but you'll be taking a message home to your friends," Sasha said, darting forward again. She was rewarded with a yelp of pain from the man as the blade sliced neatly down his side. A trickle of silver seeped from him and he glared at her.

"Either I kill you now or you walk away and tell your buddies to leave me alone," Sasha said easily, her eyes tracking his every move, waiting for the subtle hint that would telegraph his next move.

And seeing his arm jut forward with the dagger, she slid her blade neatly through the man's heart, grimacing as he dissolved in a silvery puddle on the pavement in the alleyway behind her gallery.

She'd gotten used to taking her blade everywhere with her. She hoped to figure out, one of these days, why she was being targeted by the fae, but for now, survival came first.

With a sigh, Sasha flicked her long, straight black hair over her shoulder and picked up the trash bag from where she'd dropped it when she'd first come outside. Tossing it into the dumpster, she walked backward to the door of her gallery before slipping inside and locking up behind her.

Triple locks, iron-bound, and a security alarm.

It wasn't just for the fae, but also for the valuables she housed here. Cloak & Dagger was Sasha's pride and joy and was far more than just a traditional gallery. With a focus on weaponry from every era, it housed one of the largest collections of ornate and intricately designed swords and daggers in all of Europe.

She couldn't quite say when her obsession with sharp instruments had come into play, exactly. It could have been at the tender age of four, when her father found her dancing on the counter with a knife in hand. Or it might have been when she discovered her first fencing book and taught herself with a thin stick behind the wall of the garden.

Sasha smiled as she slipped her blade into the sheath at her belt. She still remembered the first time she'd slid the foil out and brandished it in front of her. Instantly, there had been a recognition – an understanding – that she was born to wield a weapon.

What had followed that discovery was a strict study of martial arts, fencing, swordplay, and finally, an intense regimen of studies that had taken her across Europe to study ancient weaponry. Her good looks, combined with her no-nonsense manner, had opened more than one art collector's door.

And by the tender age of thirty, she'd opened her own store and become one of the leading experts in Celtic and Roman weaponry in Ireland, if not the world.

One would think her prowess with a sword would have given her fiancé pause before cheating on her.

Sasha rolled her eyes as she crossed the honey-toned wood floors of her gallery to flick the lights off in the front display windows. Pulling down the protective metal gate that secured the windows at night, she locked up and turned to look at her gallery.

Aaron had never appreciated what she'd built here.

The walls were covered with a cool gray paint color, just a hint darker than white, allowing the colors of the swords and daggers on display to pop. Sasha had created little collection areas that would walk a visitor through various eras of weaponry. The display was stunning and her store was one of her greatest accomplishments, if she did say so herself.

Aaron had sniffed at her gallery and referred to it as "Sasha's little folly." Sasha shook her head as she crossed the room, switching off lights as she went. Her hand unconsciously went to the knife sheathed at her waist as she remembered the day she'd come home early to surprise Aaron and make him a home-cooked meal for once.

Sasha huffed out a laugh.

It was all so trite and boring, really, she thought as she sat at her desk and switched her laptop on. Same old story. Finding your lover in bed with someone else.

Cheating was a coward's way out. And the last thing Sasha needed was to be hitched to a lazy cheater. It had been a blessing in disguise, though at the time, Sasha had barely restrained herself from taking a knife to his unmentionables. She snorted. *And I do mean unmentionable*, she thought.

Not that she hadn't threatened it.

The very real fear in his eyes had been enough to tame the beast inside Sasha, and she'd kicked him out that very day, and hadn't had to see him since. She couldn't say the experience had done anything to increase her willingness to trust other people again – but she was working on it.

It didn't help that silver-eyed fae had begun popping up everywhere she went, trying to kill her. That'd do something to a person's trust in pretty much everything and everyone.

Sasha leaned in to read an email she'd received from a contact at the university she'd reached out to. For a month now, she'd been trying to dig deeper into the history of the fae in Ireland and how legend was interwoven with reality. Separating fact from fiction was an almost insurmountable task, but she was chipping away at it a day at a time.

And the fact of the matter was – fae existed and they were trying to kill her.

It was enough to keep her up all night seeking answers.

# CHAPTER 2

*H*e watched her. As he always did – always had.

Declan Manchester leaned into the shadows of the alley as Sasha strode from the building at just before half one in the morning. She'd been keeping later and later hours over the past month and it was beginning to frustrate him. Didn't she know better than to walk the streets alone late at night?

The late February wind whipped around the corner of the darkened street, flipping a piece of paper into the air to flutter beneath the warm glow of a street light. Sasha strode past it, her stride long for her petite body, her head up and alert as she scanned the sidewalk. With slim black leggings tucked into no-nonsense black boots, a fitted leather jacket, and a black cap tugged low over her straight hair, she looked like she was about to rob a bank.

Or like every city-dweller walking down the street in mid-winter.

She favored black, Declan had learned through the

years. He wondered why. With her black hair and piercing blue eyes, he often wondered if color would suit her better.

But then she wouldn't be his. His fierce Sasha, clad in black, conquering challenges head-on. *His.*

His to protect.

His to know.

His for all time.

Declan straightened and followed her, keeping to the shadows and never revealing himself. The time to tell her was close – but he'd yet to figure out if he was supposed to be the one to inform her of what was going on. Trusting that the Goddess would handle it, Declan had stuck to his orders of being invisible.

The first treasure had been found. It was only a matter of time before his role with Sasha would escalate.

*Na Cosantoir* were not supposed to reveal themselves.

Their job was to protect the Seeker on her quest.

And no matter how much Declan itched to talk to Sasha, to tell her how beautiful she was, how much he admired her gallery and who she was...

It was forbidden.

# CHAPTER 3

*S*asha stepped lightly down the street that led to her small apartment. She'd learned to carry herself quietly, always listening, always scanning to see if anything triggered a warning in her brain.

Shooting a glance behind her, she studied a shadowed alley carefully before moving forward.

For a while now, she'd felt like she was being followed. Sasha just couldn't shake the itchy feeling at the back of her neck that someone was watching her every move. It was a different feeling than the one she got when the fae were trying to attack her. Those attacks happened swiftly and triggered every alarm in her being.

This feeling was… different. Comforting, almost.

And that alone should trigger a warning, Sasha thought as she unlocked her door and clattered up the dimly lit stairway to her apartment. Wanting – or needing – a false sense of comfort made her vulnerable.

And vulnerable was something that she refused to be again. She could thank Aaron for that little lesson. Sasha tossed her keys in a dish on a small table and swung her leather jacket off to hang on a hook by the door. Easy in, easy out. Triple locking her doors, Sasha turned and scanned her apartment, checking to see if any of her tells were out of place.

She always left things arranged in a certain manner when she left her apartment – a throw pillow placed at an odd angle, a cupboard door left slightly open. If someone broke in and tried to hide their tracks, they'd automatically straighten the pillow or close the cupboard door.

Seeing nothing amiss, Sasha followed the narrow hallway that led to her small bedroom. After the breakup with Aaron, she had found herself drawn to this small, quaint apartment, in direct opposition to the opulent modern penthouse that he had favored. Waste of money, Sasha thought as she flicked the light on in her bedroom and strode to her dresser. Why spend money on fancy tables and chairs when she could buy an eighteenth-century ruby-encrusted dagger?

And that was just the first of the places where she and Aaron had differed.

Sasha folded her clothes neatly and slipped a worn t-shirt over her head. Why was she even thinking of Aaron? It wasn't like she missed him.

Perhaps it was just to remind herself of her mistakes and how far she'd come, Sasha thought as she went through her evening skincare routine. Though she wasn't one for makeup, her dewy skin was a point of pride and she religiously slathered it with the best creams and serums she could afford.

She may have made a huge mistake with Aaron, but she wouldn't be so careless with her skin.

And on that note, Sasha thought as she slipped into bed, she'd do well to stay focused on the problems in her life that were bigger than a lazy cheat of an ex-boyfriend – like the email she'd scanned before she'd left work that night, from her old contact at Trinity College.

The Four Treasures Celtic creation myth.

It seemed she had more research to do.

# CHAPTER 4

The sun was struggling to peek through the gray haze of clouds that hung low over the busy streets of Dublin. Gray weather wasn't unusual to Dubliners and they hustled and bustled about their morning, clogging the sidewalks and streets on their way to work. Sasha dodged effortlessly through the people on the sidewalk, her mind focused on the contents of the email she'd received the night before.

The story wasn't that unusual. Well, perhaps it was, Sasha thought as she ducked out of the way of a man brandishing a hot cup of to-go coffee while yelling angrily into his cell phone. She just shook her head and kept moving. It wouldn't be the city if there wasn't someone having a work crisis before eight in the morning.

The Four Treasures myth was a story woven through Celtic history. It spoke of the Goddess Danu sending her children to Innisfail, also known as Ireland, with the goal of saving the land from evil fae that inhabited it. They took with them on their quest the four great treasures of the four great god cities. It was all very mythological and beautiful, heavy with history, ripe with drama and battle, as legends were wont to be.

But how that had anything to do with her current situation, Sasha couldn't quite figure out. Still, at the very least, it gave her a direction to focus upon.

"Day at a time, Sash," Sasha murmured to herself as she glanced over her shoulder before quickly unlocking the back door of her gallery and slipping inside. It had been her mantra when she'd gone through her breakup with Aaron, too. Now that fae were trying to murder her, she supposed 'a day at a time' took on a lot more meaning.

As she glanced at her collections, she was instantly soothed. There was something about being close to her swords and daggers that calmed her.

Which, she could admit, might make her sound like a nutter to some people.

Okay, most people.

But Sasha loved her gallery and the pieces of art she housed there. There was no reason to live a life lacking in passion – and her passion lay in the blade.

Sasha tossed her leather jacket over the back of her desk chair and slipped the knit cap from her hair – braided back today – then fired up her computer. She had a good two hours before she opened for the day and she was determined to make some headway on the legends. Reaching into her right drawer, she pulled out a granola bar from her stash and munched on her usual breakfast as her computer beeped about new emails.

The jangling ring of the phone on her desk startled her, and Sasha held her hand to her heart for a moment, eying the phone suspiciously. It was mighty early in the day for a phone call at the gallery. Deciding to ignore it and let it go to voicemail, she focused her eyes back on the screen.

And when the caller hung up after several rings, Sasha smiled. She'd been right not to waste time talking to a wrong number.

The phone rang again, and she raised an eyebrow at it.

"Cloak and Dagger," she answered primly, putting a hint of annoyance into her tone.

"Sasha Flanagan?" A woman's voice, bubbly and cheerful, chirped at her through the phone.

"Yes, and who is this?" Sasha asked, her eyes trailing to the dagger lying next to her computer.

Some might say she was paranoid.

Sasha preferred the term 'prepared.'

"The name's Bianca. I just wanted to check if you were in early. I must speak with you immediately," Bianca said, her voice firm, but not overly urgent.

"We don't open until ten. I'm afraid you'll have to wait. Is there a particular piece of weaponry you're interested in?"

Sasha tilted her head at the woman's chuckle.

"Seamus would be the first to tell you I'd best not be wielding too many weapons. Though I held my own, didn't I?" Bianca seemed to be talking to someone else.

"If you're not interested in what my gallery sells, perhaps you can tell me what is so urgent that you must meet with me, then?" Sasha said, her voice dripping annoyance as she ran her finger over the jeweled hilt of the dagger, the light from the lamp on her desk reflected there.

"I figured you'd want to know why fae keep trying to

kill you. But by all means – if you're too busy for that, Seamus and I will go get ourselves a full Irish over at Bee and Bun. They've got the best coff–" Bianca trailed off as Sasha interrupted her.

"Ten minutes."

"See ya soon!" Bianca chirped.

Sasha stood, sliding the dagger into her pocket and pulling open another drawer. Adrenaline pumped through her, along with a deep suspicion of the caller. It couldn't be so easy to find out what she wanted to know.

It never was.

There was always a price to pay.

In a matter of moments, Sasha was fully armed. She had knives slipped into both boots, a sword at her waist, her dagger in her pocket, knives tucked in various coat pockets, and even a small razor blade hidden away in the tie of her braid.

Though the woman's voice hadn't triggered any warnings in her head, Sasha was quite certain that she was about to walk into a trap. With that in mind, she eased herself from the building and locked up behind her. There was no way she'd allow a threat into a gallery housing hundreds of weapons that could be used against her.

Sasha was distrustful of everyone, but she wasn't stupid.

Leaning against the door and crossing her arms against her chest, she settled in to wait.

# CHAPTER 5

*I*t wasn't long before a bouncy blonde wearing a bright red coat and a blue knit cap rounded the corner. Sasha immediately dismissed her as a potential threat, but found herself straightening and sliding the dagger into her hand as her eyes landed on the man who followed a step behind the woman.

Tall and gangly, with a shock of red hair and a cool street style, he seemed like a fairly cheerful Irish bloke.

Aside from the fact that he was giving off a faint purple glow, that is.

Sasha narrowed her eyes, and found that the hue intensified when she did so.

"Sasha?" the blonde asked, stopping a few feet from her and eyeing the dagger cautiously.

"Bianca. And I'm assuming this one is the Seamus I heard about," Sasha murmured, her eyes tracking between the two. She wondered just what their game was.

Silver fae were one thing, but people glowing purple? Either the world had gone crazy, or Sasha was finally tipping over the precipice and skidding down the long steep slope into madness.

"At your service," Seamus agreed, rocking back on his heels and beaming at Sasha. It was enough to make Sasha tighten her grip on her blade and tip lightly back and forth on her feet, distributing her weight evenly so she could move quickly should she need to.

"I can't be saying I'll be needing any servicing," Sasha bit out, and Bianca let out a peal of laughter.

"I'm the only one Seamus is servicing these days, isn't that right, sweets?" Bianca said, sending a flirtatious smile over her shoulder to Seamus. Though his cheeks reddened slightly, he sent her a glowing smile before turning back to Sasha.

"My beauty is correct. That wasn't the type of service I was implying. Though I'm sure you'd have no trouble in that department should you ever need to find someone to… assist," Seamus said easily.

Bianca nodded enthusiastically. "You're right stunning, you are. I'm quite sure you have men lining up to be with you." Bianca studied the dagger in Sasha's hand and added, "Though I suggest losing the dagger. It might seem a little off-putting to some."

Sasha sighed. She'd have buried her face in her hands if she weren't currently holding a weapon.

"You wanted to see me?" Sasha said, skipping over whatever the hell they were talking about to get to the point.

"Right, we did. Though maybe we should talk inside?" Bianca suggested, shooting a glance down the alley. Though it was empty, Sasha knew that many people cut through this alley to skip the busy sidewalks of the main street.

"And let you into a shop full of weapons that could be used on me? Especially with this one?" Sasha asked, gesturing to Seamus, still glowing a light violet hue.

"What's that supposed to mean?" Bianca narrowed her eyes.

Sasha narrowed her eyes right back. Glancing left and right, she lowered her voice. "He's purple," she hissed, feeling a tinge of embarrassment trickle through her at the words.

"Duh, he's Danula." Bianca said, chuckling as though the entire world was in on some secret that Sasha had never heard of. Sasha only knew that it irritated her to feel like she was being left out of a joke – or something much larger.

Credit Aaron for that extra annoyance, Sasha thought. There was nothing she hated more, these days, than feeling like she didn't know what was going on, or that she was being played for a fool.

"And you're expecting me to be knowing what that means then?" Sasha hissed.

Bianca glanced at Seamus again. "I can't see it," Bianca mused. "But I'm not *Na Sirtheior*. Which is probably a good thing. I'm not sure if I want to see my man glowing purple, know what I'm saying?"

Sasha's hand clenched around the dagger again. She briefly thought about poking the blonde with the tip of the knife. Just enough to make her squeal, no real bodily harm, but if they didn't explain themselves shortly, Sasha was about to lose her patience.

"No, I really don't know what you're saying. At all," Sasha bit out.

Bianca sighed, rolling her eyes at Seamus. "It looks like we've got a cranky one on our hands. Have you not had coffee yet today?"

Sasha pressed her lips together and counted to ten, raising her eyes to the sky as she inhaled deeply through her nose.

"Sweets, I think she's not interested in small talk. Listen, my name's Seamus. I'm a Danula, which in other words pretty much means 'good fae.' The bad fae – those silver guys that keep trying to murder you? Yeah, we're trying to stop them from finding the Four Treasures before the year is over. And you're next up, sister, so you can wipe that look of disbelief off your face and get focused real quick."

"See? You see why I like this man? He's just so… take-charge. Bad ass. You wouldn't expect it from looking at him, but he really is. I've seen him mow down a field of Domnua – that's the silver fae to you – and I'd be lying if I said my heart didn't go pitter-pat." Bianca beamed at Sasha.

"How can I possibly know what you're saying is the truth?" Sasha sputtered. She felt like a cat backed into a corner, her hackles raised.

"I told you she wasn't going to believe us," Bianca said, reaching down for her purse. She paused when Sasha lifted her hand holding the dagger. "Calm down, killer. I'm just going to give you some information and our contact info. We're staying at a swank hotel right by here. It's like I'm on vacation in my own town! I might even get a massage!" Bianca said, holding out a small envelope.

Sasha snatched it from her hand and then motioned with the dagger. "Please leave. I'll contact you if this checks out."

"Fine by me. More time for breakfast," Bianca said cheerfully, winding her arm through Seamus's. They both turned and walked down the alley with seemingly not a care in the world. Aside from the faint tinge of purple around Seamus, they could be any random couple on a leisurely morning stroll.

Sasha's fingers dug into the envelope. Looking around quickly, she unlocked the door and slipped back into the gallery, her heart pounding in her chest.

She didn't know who – or what – she could trust.

# CHAPTER 6

*S*mart woman, Declan thought as he watched
Sasha slip back inside her gallery. He was on the
roof of the building across the alleyway. He'd staked out
the spot years ago with a quick scale up the fire escape. It
was the tallest building on the block and an ideal lookout.

Being *Na Cosantoir* afforded him a superhuman speed,
and should a Domnua sneak up on Sasha he'd be able to
drop to the ground and handle the situation very quickly.

The man with the cute blonde was the first Danula
Declan had seen in ages. He had immediately been filled
with a sense of brotherhood, as always happened when he
was near his kin. Fae were tricky like that – both fierce and
spirited, while also deeply emotional beings. Declan was
still confused as to how the Domnua could be such
murderous creatures. But he figured a couple thousand
years in the underworld would probably make even the
nicest of blokes a bit snarly.

Bianca and Seamus, he mused, pulling out his phone
and shooting off a text. It was in code, naturally, as the fae

loved electronics and could easily hack into even the highest levels of security. The code he used was known only to the Protectors.

His true brothers.

The ones who were with him on this journey, those before, and those now – tasked with protecting the Seekers. It was one of the highest honors that could be bestowed upon a Danula, and one that Declan didn't take lightly.

Declan shifted, his tall body rippling with lean muscles, like a cat stretching before it pounced. He wore his brown hair pulled back in a small nub at the base of his neck – perhaps it was vanity that caused him to leave it longer, but more often than not it was because he didn't make time for things like going to the barber. If anything, he'd hack at it with a dagger occasionally. Hazel eyes, tending mainly toward green, dominated a craggy and interesting face, and he'd been told on more than one occasion that he was hot.

Declan shook his head at the thought.

Who had time for "hot"? He was trying to keep Sasha alive and honor the Goddess Danu by finding the Sword of Light – the next treasure on their quest.

It was finally his turn – their turn – and he would let nothing stop him from protecting Sasha on her journey.

He could only hope to protect his heart along the way, too.

# CHAPTER 7

*S*asha tugged the razor blade from the hair tie in her braid, knowing that if she didn't pull it out now she'd likely forget it and slice herself later when she was pulling her braid out. Dropping the blade on the desk near the envelope, she moved to a long sideboard in her office. She slipped a key from her pocket, then unlocked a door and pulled out a slim flashlight. Switching it on, she shone the black light over the envelope, examining it for any traces of powder or tampering.

Satisfied, Sasha sat down and picked up the razor blade, neatly slicing the envelope and drawing the folded pages out. In moments, she was absorbed.

"The Seekers," Sasha muttered, leaning back and staring at a moody seascape she'd hung over her desk. It had been one of her first purchases for the gallery that wasn't a piece of weaponry, and it had pleased her to no end that she could afford it. It was painted by a brilliant artist named Aislinn, who lived on the west coast of Ireland, and there was something about the juxtaposition of the cliffs against stormy skies and raging water that spoke to her.

No peaceful sunsets for Sasha. There was always a storm raging within.

If what Bianca had written on these pages was the truth, then Sasha was about to have a storm both within and without. According to Bianca, it was their belief that Sasha was part of some mythological faction of Seekers who were tasked with finding the Four Treasures before the year was over.

If they failed, the Domnua – the bad fae of the under-world – would rise up and rule Ireland once again.

No big deal or anything.

Sasha leaned back and pulled her braid off her shoul-der, unconsciously running her hands over each dip and curve of hair, something she always did when deep in thought.

For all that Aaron had tricked her and lied to her, Sasha believed she had a fairly good bullshit meter. Or at least she'd once had – perhaps she could no longer trust her instincts. After all, she'd lived with and loved someone who had lied to her for years. Perhaps her instincts were crap.

However, the information contained here didn't read false to Sasha. Which, for some reason, made her very, very angry. Slamming her hand on the desk, she got up to pace the gallery.

Was this another situation in her life that she was a pawn in? Something she was involved in and didn't know the rules? Didn't know what game was being played? Whom could she trust – and how could she trust anyone, then? It infuriated her to know that there was a possibility she'd been a part of something much bigger and had never once been told about it.

"I mean… who does that? I'm supposed to freaking find the Sword of Light and, you know, kill off a bunch of murdering fae, but you know, we'll wait until the day of to tell you about it?" Sasha swore, long and loud, as her fury bounced off the walls of her gallery.

"I mean, that's quite possibly the shittiest way of going about recovering a treasure. There needed to be plans. And discussions. And plans," Sasha fumed, tugging her braid as she paced.

But what if this was all a joke? Maybe some elaborate thing Aaron had concocted to mess with her…

Shaking her head, Sasha resumed pacing, tucking thoughts of Aaron away as she ran through the information she'd just read. According to Bianca, Sasha was one of the Seekers, there was some sort of protector who would join her on her quest, and Bianca and Seamus would apparently tag along for the ride as well.

"You know, a squad and all." Sasha threw up her hands and went back to the desk to look at the pages. Spying a dash of red ink that formed an arrow, she flipped the last page over.

"Check under your hair. You'll be marked. It looks like this," Bianca had scrawled, and drawn a design of a Celtic quaternary knot.

"You've got to be kidding me," Sasha swore again. Then, helpless not to, she ran her fingers into her black hair, trailing them along her scalp until they slid over a minuscule raised bump at the nape of her neck. "What the…"

Sasha pulled a small mirror from her purse and moved to the bathroom tucked into the corner of the gallery. Flipping the light on, she turned and held the mirror up so she could examine the bump on her neck.

Sasha swore and leaned closer. "Sure and the saints must be deceiving me."

Sure enough, a small raised knot was etched into her scalp – almost reminiscent of a small tattoo.

A bolt of fear, mixed with anger, shot through her.

This was not how her life was supposed to go. She was supposed to continue to build her gallery and shop until it was one of the most elite in the world. Then she'd find some handsome man who worshiped her, and their pictures would be splashed across all the society pages so Aaron could see just what he'd lost.

The last thing her dream involved was to be pulled into some mad quest for treasure and saving Ireland from dark fae.

"Feck, feck, feck," Sasha swore, resuming her pacing of the gallery. She'd be lying if she said she wasn't intrigued. It was the Sword of Light, after all. That was right up her alley.

So many myths and legends wound their way around the Sword of Light, but the story that had always resonated with her was that it was the sword of truth – of justice. All other things aside, Sasha could get behind a quest for something like that.

Glancing back at the papers, a thought occurred to her.

She strode to the back door and whipped it open.

"Protector!" Sasha shouted at the top of her lungs, her voice echoing in the alleyway. When there was no response, she shouted again.

"Protector!"

"Are you out of your damn mind?"

Sasha froze. An instant before, there had been no one standing in front of her. Now her eyes trailed up denim-clad legs to broad shoulders covered in worn leather that fit like a second skin. Up, up, and further up until she found a scowling face with moody green eyes staring down at her.

Sasha paused as heat laced her belly, and her thoughts skewed immediately to anything but decent, anything but survival – which was what she should have been thinking after a strange man showed up in front of her at preternatural speed.

"Ah, so you're my Protector. Nice to meet you," Sasha said, stepping back and firmly closing the door in his face.

Leaning back against it, she covered her face with her hands while her heart pounded in her chest, reminding her that she was still alive, that everything that was happening was very much real – and that apparently she still could have lustful thoughts, on occasion.

"This is about to get real interesting," Sasha muttered and went to find Bianca's contact info.

# CHAPTER 8

"I brought you a scone. A skinny bitch like you needs to eat more."

Sasha jumped at the intrusion, her knee hitting the underside of the desk. She rubbed it furiously as she glared back at her assistant, Maddox.

"Give a girl warning, would you?"

Placing his hands on his hips, Maddox tilted his head and raised an eyebrow at Sasha, the picture of an annoyed diva.

"And what makes you think I didn't? Do I do anything quietly? Shoot, I was all but singing my way into the building, because you know I had just the best time with a delightfully delicious new specimen last night," Maddox sang, dropping the bag of food on her desk and twirling around the room, his flowy white shirt swirling around him and bracelets tinkling at his wrists.

Maddox had come to Sasha's store two years ago and insisted on working for her. Though she hadn't needed an assistant at the time, he'd quickly won her over with his off-beat charm, no-nonsense attitude, and eye for expensive things. It didn't hurt, either, that he was a natural salesman, quickly moving people past their initial surprise at his sparkly nail polish and scads of jewelry to finding themselves purchasing something they hadn't even known they'd wanted.

Sasha narrowed her eyes at Maddox as he buzzed around the room, giving her the details on his latest crush. Were her eyes playing tricks on her?

"Maddox," Sasha said, her voice sharp enough to cut through his winding story. Sure enough, there was the faintest hint of purple hovering around him.

"Yes?" Maddox asked, annoyance crossing his face briefly at being interrupted.

"You're Danula," Sasha said, her eyes trained on his. She caught it, the faint flicker in his eyes, and rose from her seat with a dagger in her hand.

"Put that knife down this instant, honey. I'm here to protect you and nothing more."

"You lied to me," Sasha seethed, stepping closer, betrayal working its way through her stomach like a burning snake.

"I had no choice," Maddox said, his hands up in front of him, his brown eyes wreathed in concern.

"Tell me how you had no choice. Explain, immediately," Sasha said, the words hissing out as the anger began to bloom within.

"It's a centuries-old curse. There are certain rules that can't be broken. One of them is that the Danula can't speak of your role until your time comes."

Sasha considered his words, her eyes never leaving his.

"Well, that's just dumb," she decided.

"I agree. I really do. I love you and I know how much you hate people who lie to you. Trust me. If I could have beheaded Aaron, I would have. But the only thing I am allowed to do is kill any Domnua if they try to get to you. I swear on everything that I love in my life." Maddox held out his bracelets and sparkly nails dramatically. "I would have told you if I could have. You're my best friend."

Sasha kept her eyes on his, her heart pounding, as she lowered the dagger.

"You have to know how this would make me feel."

"I do. I really, really do. But it was either leave you unprotected or face your wrath when you found out what I was. I'd rather you be mad at me and alive than left vulnerable."

And there you have it, Sasha thought, sheathing her dagger back at her waist. Maybe there were shades of gray when it came to lying, but that didn't mean it didn't hurt.

"I'm hurt. But I will get past it," Sasha finally said.

Maddox's eyes lit up. "You'll forgive me?"

"I… just give me a moment. I've only found out more details this morning. It's all kind of rocketing around my brain right now. I can't seem to grasp what's going on here," Sasha admitted, her hand coming unconsciously to the bump at the nape of her neck.

"Well, let's get to making sense of things. Because the clock just started," Maddox said, coming forward to touch her arm and propel her back to her desk. Pausing, he wrapped an arm loosely around her shoulder. "You know I love you."

Sasha sighed, the angry knot of betrayal loosening inside of her as she leaned briefly into his warmth.

"I know."

"Tell me everything you know. I'll fill in the holes," Maddox said, grabbing his to-go cup of coffee and kicking back into the armchair tucked by her desk. He'd sat in just that spot a thousand times over the years and Sasha couldn't help but be comforted by the familiarity of their morning routine, talking over coffee and scones, catching each other up on their personal lives. She could hold onto the hurt of being lied to… or decide to venture forward and learn more about this mythological web she was entwined in.

"Well, I called out my Protector, for one," Sasha said, leaning back in her chair.

Maddox choked on his coffee, slamming the cup down on the desk and covering his mouth as he coughed, his eyes watering. Today his platinum blond hair was gelled into a mini fauxhawk of sorts and the point of it bounced back and forth as he gasped for air.

"You all right then?" Sasha asked, leaning forward to take a sip of her own coffee.

"Just let me…" Maddox gasped and wiped his eyes, pounding his chest dramatically as he took one more deep breath. "Please elaborate on what you mean by you 'called out your Protector.'"

"Well, I learned that there's some sort of faction of Protectors who get tasked with taking care of the Seekers. Which is me, apparently. So I just went outside and yelled for him."

Maddox covered his face with both hands, breathing

deeply as he shook his head back and forth, the bracelets on his wrist jingling lightly.

"Are you out of your mind?" Maddox finally asked through his hands.

"Funny, that's what he asked me too."

"Your Protector is supposed to never reveal himself to you. It was meant that you be kept separate, so no feelings would get involved, and so they can protect you at all costs," Maddox said evenly.

"Yes, well, looks like I broke my first rule," Sasha said, shrugging one shoulder delicately. "Oops."

"Oops is right," Maddox muttered, turning to dig into the bag of scones. "I need comfort food."

"You always need comfort food," Sasha pointed out.

"Perhaps I need to be constantly comforted," Maddox shot back, waving the scone in his hand. "Preferably in the arms of someone quite handsome."

"You should meet my Protector then." Sasha winked at Maddox as she dug in the bag for her own scone.

"Ohhh," Maddox breathed, leaning in. "Tell me more."

"He's tall. Like easily a foot taller than me. Strong, but not in like an overly brute way, you know?" Sasha asked and Maddox nodded along, waving his scone at her to continue. "More like… a panther or something. He moved fast, faster than is human, and his face was all angles and mutinous green eyes. Longer hair, pulled back with a tie."

Maddox fanned his face dramatically.

"They always pick the best ones to be the Protectors."

"I wouldn't know. Care to fill me in?"

"Being a Protector is a great honor. So long as our kin has inhabited Ireland, we've known of this curse. There are hundreds of years of Protectors and Seekers, but it was all with the intent of gathering info. But in this year? This last year before the curse either ends or comes to fruition? Well, that's the time for Seekers to actually *find*. It all comes down to this. The final countdown." Maddox began to whistle the tune.

"So, no pressure then?" Sasha asked, raising an eyebrow at him.

"None at all, my love, none at all." Maddox shot her a cheeky grin.

Despite herself, Sasha found herself grinning back. She loved a challenge. "Game on then."

"That's my girl." Maddox shot her an air kiss.

# CHAPTER 9

"*N*ow just who are these two again?" Maddox sniffed as they entered a sleek hotel just ten minutes from Cloak and Dagger.

"All I know is that the guy is one of your brethren. And the blonde has a mouth on her," Sasha said. Maddox looked intrigued, but held his tongue as Sasha greeted the man behind the front desk.

They'd decided – given the circumstances – that it would be best to close the gallery for the day, if not for a while. Sasha didn't want to think about what a hit her business would take if she left the gallery closed for a few weeks. Luckily, she lived a fairly frugal life and had a sizeable nest egg in savings, but it still didn't rest easy with Sasha. She liked working – it was the one thing that truly filled her soul with happiness. Closing up shop was akin to not feeding her child.

"Saving the world here, Sash," Sasha muttered to herself as they made their way to the elevators. The modern décor of neon green and subtle gray didn't work for Sasha, and all the bright color made her want to squint. *What ever happened to good old black and white?* she wondered as they stepped into the elevator.

"Trying too hard," Maddox decided.

Sasha turned to him with a smile. "The décor?"

"Obviously," Maddox sniffed, and examined a nail. "These new places try to be so sleek and edgy. Could you imagine working around that neon green all day? I'd go blind."

"And that is why we work so well together," Sasha agreed as the doors slid seamlessly open. They stepped out into another gray and neon green hallway.

"I see the theme continues," Maddox murmured as they found the door.

They both paused as it swung open, Bianca on the other side with her hands on her hips. The blonde coolly assessed Maddox and he stepped back, doing the same to her.

"You're perfect," Bianca decided, smiling up at Maddox.

"What's perfect is your hair color, honey. Tell me where you get it done," Maddox said, like recognizing like.

"I don't. It's natural."

"No," Maddox breathed as they stepped into the hotel suite.

"I swear," Bianca said, shooting a smile over her shoulder at Sasha. Sasha tried not to feel annoyed that Maddox and Bianca had clicked so instantly.

"You've been blessed, then, that's for sure," Maddox said and Bianca all but bounced as she led them further into the suite. Seamus lounged on a long narrow gray couch that appeared to be chosen more for its aesthetic than its comfort.

"Brother," Maddox said immediately, bowing his head slightly to Seamus. Seamus stood up, holding out both of his hands for a complicated handshake that moved so quickly that Sasha could barely follow it.

"Secret Boy's Club handshake?" Sasha asked, raising an eyebrow at the two.

Bianca swept an accusing look at Sasha as the men smiled. "You didn't tell me you had a Danula already."

"I didn't know I did have one …" Sasha's voice trailed off and she tugged at the end of her braid, a sure sign of annoyance which Maddox immediately picked up on.

"Why don't I pour us a cup of tea and we'll just settle in for a quick chat," Maddox said, moving to the side table where a nice spread of biscuits and fruits was arranged with style.

Sasha perched herself warily on the edge of a gray chair with neon green flecks scattered throughout the cushion fabric. Had the decorator really not considered any other colors? She waved away a cup of tea and leveled a stare at Bianca.

"Well? You have me here."

Bianca raised an eyebrow at Maddox, who just shrugged at her.

"Well, aren't you just a ball of sunshine and roses?" Bianca said, sniffing a bit as she leaned back into the couch, where Seamus automatically put his arm around her shoulders. Sasha studied them both carefully, memorizing the way Bianca's eyes slanted just a bit at the corners, and how Seamus's hair was just the perfect Irish red. It was an old habit of hers – sizing others up quickly and remembering nuances most would forget. It helped to study faces when fencing – or frankly, in any hand-to-hand combat, Sasha thought as she idly tapped her finger on her leg. People will communicate their next move quite clearly with the smallest of tells.

"Sunshine and roses doesn't win battles," Sasha pointed out, and scrunched her nose when Maddox glared at her. "What? I'm just saying."

"Well, now that the niceties are done with, let's get to it, shall we?" Bianca said, the slightest bit of bitchiness entering her tone as she smoothed her hands over her pants. "It's your turn to find one of the four treasures, which we all know as the Sword of Light – or Sword of Truth, however you want to look at it – from various myths and legends. I prefer the Sword of Truth myself, but that's just a personal opinion."

"Why?" Sasha asked, relaxing a little as Bianca's face became animated with her lecture.

"The most basic retelling of the Four Treasures Celtic creation myth holds that the Sword was a sword of light and could destroy anything the wielder wished. However, I've read different iterations through many texts that also suggest it was a sword of truth or justice. It was said that when the rightful owner held it, not only could it cleave any man's or fae's head straight from their body, but also it would not leave the holder's side. It was a useful tool for the great rulers to use in battle as nobody could win against it."

"So it's steel? This sword?" Sasha asked.

Bianca paused and considered her words. "I did say it was steel, or didn't I? Are swords made from other materials?"

"Depends on the clan, the era, and the craft. In theory, a sword can be made from many materials. Are there any identifying marks I should be aware of?" Sasha asked.

"It's fae, though. It's magickal. Does that mean it would still be steel?" Bianca asked, and Sasha paused.

"I can't quite say as I know the answer to that. I haven't really believed in magick in my life, up until fae started showing up and trying to kill me."

"How long has that been going on?" Seamus interjected.

"A few months, if not longer," Maddox said, easing onto the couch with a perfectly balanced cup of tea in his right hand. "I've taken care of the stray few, and I'm sure her Protector has as well. But she's handled more than she should have had to on her own."

Had anyone looked in on them, the group would have seemed to be having an easy chat over scones and tea – perhaps planning for an afternoon tour of a museum, or a pub crawl of the Temple Bar district. Instead, they spoke of magick and beheadings, good fae and bad fae, as easily as if they were discussing what the weather held for the next day.

"The sword? What does it look like? When was it last seen? What do you know about it?" Sasha fired off the questions in rapid order, dismissing the discussion of her having to kill fae. There was nothing to discuss – a problem had arisen and she'd taken care of it. Period. That's how she lived her life.

"We know it has a quaternary knot at the base," Seamus said, pulling Bianca's hand into his lap to shush her. Sasha caught the annoyed look that ran across Bianca's face, but was impressed with the blonde's ability to keep her mouth shut when necessary. "And that the knot is made of four metals – copper, silver, gold, and platinum. They all intertwine to make a beautiful mark – one that is said to glow when the rightful owner holds it."

"A Celtic knot design like the one on my neck?" Sasha asked.

Seamus nodded. "Yes, four corners to the knot. Four treasures. Four Seekers. Four Protectors."

"And four months," Bianca added, her chin lifting a bit, "Four months to find the sword."

"And you said the stone has been found? How long did that take?"

Bianca brightened at that, her round body all but vibrating with excitement as she launched into the tale of a woman named Clare climbing Mt. Brandon and banishing the Domnua to the depths before returning with the stone. It was quite the tale, and Bianca related it with a flair that told Sasha she was used to storytelling.

"So we're winning right now? And the baton's been passed to me?" Sasha asked.

Bianca beamed at her. "Precisely. So I think we should make an action plan," Bianca began and Sasha held up her hand, bringing Bianca's flow of words to a halt.

"There's no 'we.' I. *I* will come up with an action plan. Is there anything else you can tell me that I need to know about this? Any clues? The last known spot for a sighting of this sword?" Sasha asked briskly, not caring that Bianca now scowled at her.

"Ah, I believe it was at a castle outside Killarney. Well, what was a castle. It's now naught but ruins, I'm certain," Seamus said quickly, squeezing Bianca's hand tightly in his own.

"Name?" Sasha asked. Maddox sighed, shaking his head at her. She didn't dignify him with a response.

"I only know it by its fae name," Seamus said. "But I can't be certain the locals would even refer to it as that now."

"Anything else I should know before I go?" Sasha said as she stood. Bianca's mouth dropped open, then she snapped it shut and stood as well, putting her hands on her hips.

"We're here to be helping you then, not your servants who just spit out whatever answers you need." Bianca huffed as she worked up a good head of mad. "There's a lot you should know. Like how to kill fae and what your magickal power is, and where to look for clues and how to identify the bad guys—"

"I've killed fae. I prefer a sword straight through the heart. But iron suffices as well. And now I know the good ones are purple and the bad ones are silver. As for clues, you haven't given me anything besides the maybe-name of a location. As for my magickal power, I'm quite certain it's not putting up with anyone's bullshit. Anything else?" Sasha said smoothly, dismissing the hurt that sliced across Bianca's face.

As far as she was concerned, the fewer people on her journey, the fewer she was responsible for keeping alive.

Hurt feelings were nothing compared to death, and Sasha didn't want anyone's blood on her hands.

Except for the fae who kept trying to kill her.

"No?" Sasha asked into the silence, then turned to Maddox. "I'm leaving. It's probably best if you stay as well. I know you're supposed to be my trusty steed and all, I doubt there is much that you can do at this point. Let's just leave the protecting to the infamous Protector, shall we?"

Sasha wanted to close her eyes so as not to witness the expression on Maddox's face, and the little clutch in her gut told her that her hurtful words had struck home. Surveying the shocked expressions on the faces in the room and weighing the icy silence that met her, she considered her work done.

Turning, she walked quickly from the room, her back straight and her stomach in knots.

"You'll be needing us! You shouldn't turn your back on your friends," Bianca called after her.

"Friends? I don't even know you."

## CHAPTER 10

"What a…" Bianca trailed off as Seamus tightened his hand on hers, his barely perceptible nod in Maddox's direction reminding Bianca that now wasn't the time for her opinions of Sasha.

"I apologize for Sasha's behavior," Maddox said stiffly, his face almost as white as his shirt.

"Ah, man, think nothing of it. You've done a wonderful job of being an added layer of protection for her. Seems to be a bit of a prickly type, I'm seeing," Seamus said, his tone cheerful as he sipped his tea. "Can't imagine it's been easy, being her friend."

"She's not all that bad," Maddox said, his face relaxing a bit as he leaned back, "In fact, she's one of my favorite people."

"Why do I find that hard to believe?" Bianca said.

Maddox laughed. "Sasha's a fierce one, but she's had to be. She's had a rough time of it. Everything she's ever done in her life she's had to fight for – from making her way in a male-dominated field, to earning the credibility and the money to open her gallery, to kicking her cheating ex to the curb. Things got a little dicey after that, you know, and her walls went way up."

"Well, that's just shite," Bianca said, her expression softening. "I hate liars."

"I'd never lie to you, my beauty," Seamus said immediately, and leaned over to kiss Bianca's cheek. Bianca dimpled up at him and then turned her attention back to Maddox.

"Sasha lives her life by a strict code of honor, most likely from the countless hours of martial arts training she's had. To deal with a liar, and something as intimate as that… well, it's the first time I've really seen her crack."

"I hope she used her martial arts skills on him," Bianca muttered.

"I hoped she would as well, but she didn't. She took the high road and very calmly moved on. Though he begged for her, she simply ignored his pleas. It was as though once he'd crossed that line… well, it was almost as if he had never existed for her. And yet, that's not totally so. Because I've yet to see her willing to trust someone since. Though lord knows I've tried to set her up. Her walls are up, that's for sure." Maddox sighed.

"So what was that little act she just pulled then?" Bianca asked.

"Well, Maddox is one of her best friends. The only reason she'd be mean to him like that is if she's trying to push him away. And based on what he just told us, there are only two reasons she'd push him away," Seamus said, holding up two fingers.

"Because she's scared of being hurt…" Bianca trailed

off and then snapped her fingers. "Or that we'll get hurt. Which in turn hurts her."

"Shite," Maddox said, and buried his face in his hands.

"Psh, now, that's nothing. We just battled a mountain of Domnua. Sasha's no match for us," Bianca said and gestured for Maddox to stand. "Up, up. Let's go now. She's got a lead on us, but we'll track her."

"Aye, we will."

# CHAPTER 11

*S*asha strode down the sidewalk, her expression mutinous, or so she surmised by the way people stepped from her path. A hint of sun poked from the clouds, the promise of spring caught in the damp wind. Not yet, Sasha thought as she sniffed the air. No, not even close to spring.

A faint flicker of silver caught her eye as she passed an alley and without hesitation she turned to stalk it down. What better way to work off this sick feeling in her gut than to kill a few fae? After all, they were the cause of her current anger. Sasha enjoyed swift and direct justice – and in this case, appropriate.

Three of them lurked by a dumpster, looking for all the world like some punk kids stealing a smoke, except for the faint silver glow that emanated from them. Sasha narrowed her eyes as she homed in on their movements, each fae straightening slightly but still pretending nonchalance.

"Hey, got a smoke?" Sasha called, putting a friendly smile on her face as she pretended to fumble in her purse.

"I've got a light in here somewhere." She palmed a razor-thin blade in her hand and smiled brightly at the fae.

"Sure," one of them mumbled. The other two looked delighted as they moved closer to her, fanning out a bit so they flanked her, while she rocked lightly back on her heels, her eyes tracking their every movement.

The first one was dead before he hit the ground, his lunge having been anticipated by the way his eyes had feinted left just before he'd moved. She barely had a moment to take another breath before the other two were upon her. Sasha grunted as one punched her in the stomach, but she'd seen the move and allowed it. Swinging the blade with her as she grunted, Sasha made quick work of the second one, slicing cleanly through his heart. Both fae evaporated in a puddle of silver, leaving only one to dance lightly in front of her, moving at inhuman speed.

Sasha's heart pounded as the Domnua bounced about, shrieking at her in an unintelligible language. Right as he went to pounce, he disappeared in a poof of silver that left Sasha's hand dangling in the air, her blade ready.

"What?" Sasha exclaimed, whirling, knife up, to confront what was behind her.

"Careful," Declan said, snatching her wrist and stopping it inches from where it wanted to pierce his throat.

A storm cloud raged across his handsome face as he glowered down at her, his entire body radiating anger.

"Don't sneak up on a girl like that," Sasha warned, and pulled her arm back, determinedly ignoring the warmth that raced up her arm from where his fingers pressed to her skin. A touch shouldn't affect her so, she thought dimly, as he refused to let go of her arm.

"Are you out of your mind?" Declan asked, still holding her arm, his tone murderous, the green of his eyes seeming to darken in his rage.

A shiver raced through Sasha, and it wasn't from the wind that had picked up, blowing a loose strand of hair around Declan's chiseled jaw. She fought an irresistible urge to reach up and tuck it behind his ear, to run her fingers over the sharp line of his jaw.

And just what was wrong with her? Sasha tried once again, unsuccessfully, to jerk her arm back. Mortified, she glared up at him.

"That's the second time you're asking me that question," Sasha pointed out, tugging again at her wrist. "You're hurting me."

As soon as she said the words, he dropped her arm, cursing long and low as he paced in front of her. Sasha took the moment to palm her blade and watch Declan pace.

Oh yeah, Maddox would faint, Sasha thought as she took in all the details she could. A fallen angel, she finally decided. His moody looks, chiseled jawline, and perfectly muscled body made her think of a depraved angel.

When he slanted an angry look at her again, Sasha quickly amended the thought. This man was no angel.

"It calls to mind a madwoman, it does. One who willingly confronts Domnua? One who calls out her Protector? Yes, I've been assigned to protect a madwoman. 'Tis the only answer," Declan said.

Sasha rolled her eyes. "I'm not mad. I'm quite simply someone who can take care of herself. Now that I'm aware of the problem, I'll take care of it," Sasha said, facing Declan.

"You… you… you'll just take care of it?" Declan sputtered, his hands clenching into fists as he looked at her in disbelief.

"Yes. I'll find the sword, hand it over, and be done with this." Sasha shrugged.

"By yourself?"

"Aye, by myself. It's a good thing you showed up, I suppose. I won't be needing your services. You're dismissed," Sasha said, tossing him a haughty glare before turning on her heel to stride from the alley.

But she let out a gasp as he appeared, as if by magick, directly in her path, causing her to slam into his muscled chest.

"Ow," Sasha exclaimed, attempting to bring her hand up to rub her nose. But instead she found her arms pinned at her sides by a very angry and very sexy male.

"You are not the Goddess. I take orders only from her. Are we clear?" Declan said softly, his words deathly serious.

Sasha found herself lost for a moment, his lips enticing her to just lean in for a little nip. Christ, what was wrong with her? She shook her head and glared up at him, mustering her best angry face while being held pinned to his body.

"Since I'm not familiar with your goddess, I can't really say whether you should be listening to her or not. But I can tell you that you can stay out of my way. I'll handle this on my own. The last thing I want or need is anyone to get hurt because of me. Including you, for what it's worth," Sasha spat. She could've kicked herself when she saw the tight lines around his mouth soften.

"It's my job to worry about you," Declan said, reaching a hand up to tug lightly at her braid. The touch spoke of an intimacy that Sasha wasn't comfortable with, and she once again tried to shift out of his arms.

"And it's my job to make sure that nobody gets killed because I've been dragged into some asinine mission outside my own control... Would you stop that?" Sasha demanded, annoyed at the grin that now rested so comfortably on his handsome face. When he scowled Declan held a dangerous look that appealed to her baser instincts, but when he smiled?

She could lose herself.

"I don't think I realized what a tender side you had," Declan murmured, and shocked her by running the pad of his thumb over her lip. Heat exploded everywhere in her body and god help her, she wanted to let out the softest of moans.

Instead she did what any woman would have done in the situation – well, any woman who was her.

She kicked him in the shins and ran.

# CHAPTER 12

*T*he scratchy sound that left Declan's throat startled him. Was he laughing? He couldn't remember the last time he had laughed. By the Goddess, what spirit Sasha had!

His pint-sized warrior, the woman of his dreams, the reality in the flesh – Declan had been besotted with Sasha since the instant he'd laid eyes on her. Her fierce exterior belied a molten inner core that showcased a heart as pure as gold.

Declan had watched her over the years, doing everything in his power not to beat up that worthless excuse for a human she'd once dated. Aaron had never been good enough for Sasha, and it had made Declan cringe every time he'd had to watch the two of them together.

He wouldn't say he was happy that Aaron had broken her trust, but at least it had taken care of that problem. Sasha had handled it like she did everything else in her life – with a steel backbone and unfailing dignity.

Declan laughed again and shook his head, running his

hand over the scruff at his jaw as he thought about her. There wasn't a definitive point that he could identify as the moment he'd fallen in love with her. He just knew it was so – sure as the rains came to Ireland, his heart would belong to no other.

Declan cursed again, tuning into his internal sixth sense until he could track her in his mind. In moments, he'd caught up to her, but stayed far back, knowing she would be infuriated if she knew he was following her.

Sasha still didn't understand how this worked. He'd follow her until his last breath, protect her at all costs, and love her through every temper tantrum or kick in the shins she delivered.

Even if it was against the rules.

# CHAPTER 13

*S*asha bit down the emotions that threatened to rise in her chest as she all but ran toward her gallery. Now was not the time for feelings, but for thinking – strategizing. As far as Sasha was concerned, she was now at war.

Which meant she had to protect her loved ones at all costs – and any others who might be collateral damage. This was her burden to bear and she would handle it with as little damage to others as possible.

Sasha's eyes darted back and forth as she stepped to the back of her gallery. Spotting no sign of silver, she punched in her code, disengaged the locks, and swung inside, quickly slamming and locking the door behind her.

"Think. What do you need?" Sasha said out loud, surveying her gallery and letting her mind dart quickly through her mental inventory. She knew she had but minutes before the Domnua would be upon her. She might as well be a sitting duck.

Sasha raced to the closet in her office and pulled out a

survival pack. She kept one packed at all times with the bare necessities and a few weapons. Sasha had seen enough zombie movies to know that it didn't hurt to be prepared. Maybe it was ridiculous, but she was praising herself now as she sprinted around the gallery, gathering various knives and daggers to add to her bag.

A glimmer of light caught her eye from across the gallery, giving her pause. Slowly, she padded across the dark room and stood in front of one of her favorite pieces.

A slim thread of light from the security camera gleamed off the hilt of an eighteenth-century Celtic embossed dagger. It was a perfectly balanced blade, with intricate designs crossing the hilt and leading to a single emerald stone centered in the middle. The stone was what had gleamed in the light. Sasha reached out, removing the blade carefully from the casing that held it affixed to the wall.

The instant the dagger touched her hand, a current of energy ran through Sasha's arm and straight to her core. She tilted her head at the dagger, studying it carefully as she weighed it in her hand. It felt right... almost as if it had been made for her.

"Now you're just being ridiculous. All this fae talk has you being fanciful now," Sasha said. But that didn't stop her from strapping the dagger to her leg, tucked neatly above her boot.

With one final look around the gallery, she closed her eyes.

"Goddess... if you are real, I only ask that you protect this space and all the antiquities I've worked so hard to assemble. I'm leaving now and will lead the Domnua away from it. Please keep this space safe."

Sasha felt foolish asking for help, even from an unknown and omnipotent being. Slinging the pack over her shoulders and buckling it to her waist, she zipped her leather jacket tight and slipped from the back door without a backward glance.

And stepped into mayhem.

# CHAPTER 14

*S*asha sent up a brief prayer of thanks for heavy doors that slammed shut because the Domnua were upon her the moment she stepped outside. After finishing packing up, she'd anticipated this, and had slipped the dagger from her boot in the seconds before she'd stepped outside.

Sasha felled three without taking a breath, the dagger sliding through them and leaving silvery puddles in its wake. She had a brief moment to marvel at the slickness of the blade before she was tackled from above.

"Damn it!" was all she could think as she automatically dove into a roll. She'd watched enough scary movies to know that she was supposed to look up. It was always the dumb girl wandering in the woods who never looks up in the trees that gets nailed. And here she was being one of those dumb girls by not even scanning her surroundings.

Not like she'd had much time, she thought, as she rolled and automatically brought her knee up between her attacker's legs, momentarily crippling him enough to slide the dagger straight into his heart. Sasha twisted, just missing the plop of silver goo as he disintegrated before her eyes. Thank goodness, she thought as she leaped to her feet. She wasn't entirely sure if silver goo would come out of leather.

Then there was no time for thought as the Domnua converged on her, one line after another. Sasha's heart pounded in her chest as she ducked, rolled, and lashed out over and over. In moments, silver dripped from every surface behind the gallery, and still they came.

It was at this moment that Sasha finally realized how grossly unprepared she was for the handling of this. Perhaps she'd grown cocky, knowing she could take down a fae or two on her own. But an army?

She was screwed.

But one thing she'd refuse to have said about her is that she went down without a fight. As adrenaline coursed through her system, she whirled to stab another one, and gasped as he melted before her dagger had even grazed his skin. Panting, she met a pair of sunny blue eyes.

"Looks like you're handling this real great on your own, champ. Why don't you let us help you out a bit?" Bianca asked cheerfully, as she turned and quickly gutted another Domnua. Sasha turned, pushing hair that had come loose from her braid from her eyes to see Maddox, Seamus, and Declan all battling the Domnua until, in moments, none remained.

Silence filled the alley, except for their panting breaths, as they surveyed the rapidly disappearing silver blood that coated the ground.

"So?" Bianca demanded, hands back on her hips, and a defiant lift to her chin.

Despite herself, Sasha found herself grinning at the chubby blonde.

"You're all right, lass. I'll be honored to have you on my team."

Bianca sniffed and idly checked her nails for any chips. "Is that you asking for our help then?"

Sasha looked briefly to the sky, biting back the snotty retort that hung on her tongue. She deserved this.

"Yes. Would you please help me find the sword?" Sasha said, refusing to look at Declan.

"I thought you'd never ask! Seamus, get the car."

"Aye, my love, anything for you."

"That was some fight, wasn't it? Do you think their blood comes out of suede? I knew I should've changed my boots," Bianca chattered, looking down at a smear of silver that marred her honey-brown boots.

In that moment, Sasha realized just how much she liked the blonde. "Most women would be having a fit right now," Sasha said, and Bianca looked at her in confusion as they walked toward the entrance of the alley to meet Seamus.

"About the boots? Ah, well, there is bound to be some damage in battle," Bianca said, shrugging it off.

"No," Sasha said with a laugh, "not about the shoes." She gestured to the alleyway behind them. "About all this. The battle. Killing fae. Not squealing and running in fear."

"Not my style. There's a lot you have to learn about me. But the first thing you should know," Bianca said, leveling her with a cool stare, "is that the Goddess Danu specifically anointed me to help others on this quest. When a Goddess has faith in you, well, it's easy to go kick some ass. Now, let's find this damn sword."

The blonde hopped into the front seat of the car under an approving nod from Maddox. Shaking her head just a bit, Sasha slid into the middle seat and found herself pressed closely against Declan's muscled body.

"You were right... he is yummy," Maddox whispered in her ear. Sasha could have sworn she heard Declan chuckle under his breath. Biting back a groan, she closed her eyes and let her head loll back against the seat. She was asleep in minutes.

# CHAPTER 15

*S*asha awoke and immediately stiffened, internally cringing as she realized that she was curled into Declan's side, his arm thrown loosely over her shoulder. Straightening, she met his eyes for a second, and the intensity she saw there made her mouth go dry.

"Um, sorry. I didn't mean to… um, sorry," Sasha said, and pulled abruptly away from him. His arm still rested on her shoulders and the heat that slid through her body just from his casual touch on her neck was making her think about things that had very little to do with their mission.

And everything to do with a different kind of mission.

"Sleeping Beauty is awake." Bianca turned and flashed her a smile, her eyes bright with a knowing look as she surveyed Declan's arm thrown over Sasha's shoulder.

"Sorry about that. I tend to fall asleep in cars, but typically only need a short amount of sleep to recharge," Sasha said as she removed Declan's arm from around her neck with a glare.

He shot her a look under heavy-lidded eyes that had

her brain scrambling for a moment, then she sneered at him in response.

Bianca watched the entire exchange with a delighted look on her face.

"Knock it off," Sasha grumbled, and both Maddox and Bianca chuckled.

It was probably just because she hadn't slept with anyone in a while. Women have needs, Sasha thought, a grumpy expression on her face. Declan was sexy. It was quite simple. No need for either of these two to be reading anything more into it.

"You know," Bianca said, turning to smile at Seamus, "Clare and Blake ended up together."

Sasha buried her face in her hands and groaned, ignoring Declan's low rumble of laughter at her side.

"Can we just not do this? I have bigger things to worry about than sex."

The word 'sex' hung in the air as everyone grew quiet.

"Can't think of a much better thing to occupy your mind with than sex," Seamus remarked cheerfully and the car erupted in laughter. Even Sasha finally broke out in a smile.

"Fair enough. Can we move on? Where are we going? What do we know? How does this work?"

"Well, last time we had a clue. Do you have any clues?" Bianca asked.

Sasha just looked at her for a moment. "I can't honestly say that I do."

"Nothing? No poems? No notes? No weird sensations or drawn to any weird objects?"

"Just my dagger," Sasha said automatically, then paused.

"Let's see," Bianca demanded, and Sasha slipped it out of her boot and handed it off to Bianca.

"So Declan," Maddox began, leaning forward a bit to look at Declan, and Sasha barely restrained herself from rolling her eyes. "Tell us about yourself."

Declan leaned forward and smiled at Maddox.

"I'm *Na Cosantoir*," Declan said simply.

"Well, yeah, duh. We know that. But like, what about you? Where are you from, what do you like doing? Do you have family?" Maddox asked, his arms crossed over his chest.

"I have family, a brother and a sister. Both of my parents are still living," Declan said, then closed his mouth.

"Chatty one, aren't you?" Maddox commented.

"I'm not here to chat. In fact, I shouldn't even be in this car. The code is that I'm supposed to remain unseen. Yet, this one here had other ideas in her head," Declan said, annoyance lacing his voice.

"Not everything can go the way you want it to," Sasha grumbled.

"Nothing's gone the way I want it to since I've laid eyes on you," Declan said, turning to stare out the window. Maddox pounced on that.

"And how long has it been since you laid eyes on our beautiful Sasha?"

Sasha rolled her eyes at that. She'd take 'striking' or 'unique' – but being called 'beautiful' always made her feel a bit squirmy. She'd fought too hard to be taken seriously in her field, and often found the terms 'pretty' or 'beautiful' to be used in a condescending manner by colleagues.

"For a handful of years," Declan said.

Sasha's brain almost shorted out. "What?" she exclaimed, swinging to punch him in the arm. "You've been following me for years? Years! And you've never said a word to me? That's stalking, you know?"

Declan just shook his head and ran his hand over the stubble on his jaw.

"It's not stalking if I'm saving your life."

"I thought this all just started recently. Why the need to watch me for so long?" Sasha demanded. Her thoughts skidded over all the years she'd owned the gallery, her time with Aaron, her travels. Just how often had he watched her and what had he watched her doing? It was a decidedly creepy feeling to know that your every move had been cataloged by a third party for years.

She wondered if he liked her.

What a stupid thing to think, Sasha admonished herself. His job wasn't to like her – his job was apparently to keep her alive and safe from the murdering fae that kept showing up at her back door. That was it. He didn't have to like her to do his job.

"Fae are tricky. They slip through and try to derail the Seekers. It's how it has always been. It's quite an honor to be chosen."

"How are you chosen?" Maddox asked.

"The Goddess chooses. It's a birthright. The mark appears and it is so," Declan said.

"You have the same mark as the Seekers?" Sasha asked, turning to look him over.

"Yes, but inverted. Just here," Declan said, turning his wrist over to show what looked like a small tattoo on the interior of his wrist.

Sasha was about to ask another question, but Bianca interrupted her. "Speaking of birthrights," she said, and held up the dagger. "Did you tell me where you got this? There's an inscription just here."

"There is?" That sincerely shocked Sasha. She was so careful with cataloging the details of every antique that came into the gallery. There was no way she would have missed an inscription.

*One must first know the dark to see the light.*

"Seriously?" Sasha asked, pulling the dagger from Bianca's hand to examine the small line of text on the hilt of the sword, winding around one of the engravings. "How did I miss this? My attention to detail is usually fantastic."

"'Tis true, my love, 'tis true. But this is fae," Maddox said, pulling the dagger gently from her hand. "Riddles, inscriptions, runes – all of those things will show up in their own time."

"Sasha, where were you born?" Bianca interrupted again.

Sasha looked at her in confusion. "What does that have to do with anything?"

"We found clues at Clare's birthplace. We might as well start at the beginning again, no?" Bianca asked, shrugging a shoulder.

Sasha felt annoyed, as she did every time this topic came up. "I was an orphan. A foster family took me in.

They didn't really know how to parent a child like me and I left as soon as I was old enough to earn a wage," Sasha said quickly, hoping that would be the end of the inquiry.

"Wait, what? You just left? What did you do?"

"Cleaned dishes, worked a library, cleaned some houses, babysat." Sasha shrugged it off. "Those types of jobs, until I was able to go on to school."

"What were your parents like?" Bianca asked.

"This doesn't matter," Sasha said, and there was a silence in the car. Sasha sighed and tugged on her braid. Maddox patted her leg in reassurance. "Listen, they're fine people. They just didn't know how to parent a child like me. They were so authoritarian, and if I didn't fall in line with their beliefs or behavior, I was cast as the black sheep. Instead of giving me the chance to learn and grow freely, they ruled with an iron hand. Unfortunately, that doesn't work well with someone like me. We clashed a lot. I think they were just as relieved to see me go as I was to say goodbye to them."

"I'm sorry, honey. That sounds awful," Bianca said, her expression soft with empathy.

"It is what it is. I just wish they had seen me for who I am instead of trying to make me into what they wanted me to be. It would have made life significantly easier. Of course, I was blamed for the arguments and the fighting, so it was easy for them to cast me in the role of the black sheep – of always being the bad one. And at this point in my life, it doesn't really matter anymore. For a long time, I still sought their approval. I wanted them to be proud of me. Now? Well, I'm living for me and I'm proud of who I am and who my friends are. I'm a good person," Sasha said, surprised to find the old angst boiling up inside her.

"Of course you are. You're one of the best people I know," Maddox said automatically.

"Thanks, but I think you may be biased. I'm not always all that nice," Sasha said with a sigh, wanting to change the conversation. "Anyway, the papers that came with me from the orphanage say I was found near to Killarney."

"Shall we head that way?" Seamus asked.

Sasha sighed again and tugged her braid.

"If we must go back to the beginning, then we go back to the beginning."

# CHAPTER 16

s the car cruised along a coastal road, Sasha went quiet and let the chatter flow around her. She didn't much like thinking of her childhood, let alone of the days before she went into the orphanage. Vague images of a woman surrounded by a glow of light, as if she were looking down at Sasha with the sun beaming behind her head, and a sense of warmth. After that, just vague images of a dark room, being hungry, and being totally out of control until she landed in a foster home.

It was one of the things that had drawn her into the martial arts world – being in control. After her erratic upbringing, control was vitally important to Sasha.

"Is there anything in particular that pops into your head when you think about the sword and your upbringing? Any connection you see?" Bianca asked, rousing Sasha from her reverie.

"That love is conditional," Sasha said automatically, and then paused. Maddox reached over and squeezed her hand, but said nothing.

"Oh, honey, do you really believe that?" Bianca's face was wreathed in sorrow and Sasha had to call on her deepest reserves to keep her walls up.

"It is, though," Sasha insisted, shrugging a shoulder. "However, I'm not sure what that has to do with the sword."

"Why do you say it is?" Seamus asked, his voice only holding curiosity, not judgment.

"It's just the way it is," Sasha said, struggling to articulate her feelings. "If you don't change yourself for the people who love you – if you don't become what they want you to be – they take their love from you. If you aren't the perfect daughter or the perfect wife, they don't love you. It's a condition of their love. It's not that uncommon, I'm not even sure why you're surprised at this. People hold expectations of others all the time. When you constantly fail to meet them, they withdraw their love. That's just how it works."

Sasha felt all that old angst swirl around in her stomach, burning a hole, desperately trying to claw its way out. Her hand clenched unconsciously around the dagger and a tingling sensation burned through her, up her arm, and shot a bolt straight into the roof of the car.

Sasha froze, staring at the singed mark in the fabric of the ceiling. Maddox swore and batted the fire out, Bianca screeched, and Seamus swung the car to the side of the road. The only one who was calm was Declan, who leveled an unreadable look at her.

Sasha closed her eyes against the tears that suddenly threatened.

She hadn't cried in years. But here she was, about to

lose the few people who claimed to be on her side. She supposed it was to be expected. You couldn't shoot a fireball through someone's car ceiling and think people would stick around.

Where had that come from, anyway? Since when could daggers shoot fire? Sweat broke out across Sasha's hairline, trickling down her neck into her braid. She kept her eyes closed, holding the tears back through sheer force of will.

Sasha jolted as she felt Declan's arm go over her shoulders, pulling her into him. She wanted to snuggle right up, bury her face in his neck, and cry it all out. All the years of pain, of feeling like the only person on her own private island, of being strong all the time against those who always sought to change her or castigate her because she was different.

A tap on her knee made her open her eyes to see Bianca smiling at her.

"Can I just say, that was pretty badass."

And despite herself, Sasha found herself laughing so hard that the tears came after all. But this time they were from the joy of finding people who accepted her.

eclan dug his nails into his palm as he looked out the window and away from where Sasha wiped tears from her eyes. He wanted to punch something or someone – take down a Domnua or two. When he'd heard the crack in her voice when she'd tried to calmly explain that love was conditional, he had been filled with anger.

Her wounds ran deep, perhaps much deeper than he had realized. No wonder she was so fierce in her day-to-day life. Not only was she a warrior, but she was protecting her heart.

It was far easier to keep a wall up than it was to let people in, then have them abandon you.

Declan knew all about walls. He'd been traveling alone for years, protecting Sasha, maintaining minimal contact with his family and his friends. It was more for preservation and dedication to the role entrusted to him than by choice; however, his solitary and introverted nature now felt normal to him. No friends meant no distractions, and he could honor the Goddess by keeping Sasha alive.

Declan slid a quick glance at Sasha and then back out the window.

He made a vow to himself in that moment. If – no, *when* they found the sword and the mission was over, he'd show Sasha the truth of unconditional love until his dying breath.

His service to the Goddess and the Danula would be over.

And he'd be free to love the one woman who'd gotten past his walls without even trying.

# CHAPTER 18

"Clare could freeze time. Well, not time, but the Domnua. And Sasha shoots firebolts. I wonder if all the powers will be elemental," Bianca mused as they wound their way toward the village where Sasha believed she had been born. Declan kept his gaze steady out the window. Sasha wondered what he was thinking about, or if he thought differently of her because of her newly discovered magickal power.

"How do you even know they all get to have powers?" Maddox inquired.

Bianca paused as she considered. "I don't. I guess I'm just hoping they do. Because, duh, how cool would that be? I mean, I know all of you are fae and this magick stuff is like, the norm, for you guys. But for me? It's like I'm living out all the myths and fairytales I've learned and lecture about. It's just beyond awesome, in my opinion. Yup, I definitely hope everyone gets magick powers." Bianca's enthusiasm was contagious and Sasha found herself relaxing back into the seat.

"You're awfully quiet," Sasha commented, nudging Declan.

"Keeping watch," Declan said, not sparing her a glance.

Sasha straightened a bit, turning to crane her head to look out the back window. "Do you think they'd ambush us?"

"Yes," Bianca and Seamus both exclaimed at once.

"I hadn't even considered that," Sasha admitted, feeling a bit foolish for thinking they were safe once they'd exited Dublin.

"We're at war. You're never safe – from here on out. Do you understand me? There's no sneaking off alone, no using the bathroom alone, nothing." Declan ordered, his green eyes hard as he stared her down.

"Yes, Captain," Sasha said, giving him a little attitude.

She was met with a stony glare.

"Tough crowd," Sasha murmured and was delighted to see a quick smile flash across Declan's face before he went back to scanning the hills.

"Turn here," Sasha said, seeing a small lane that jutted from the main road. She had no idea why she insisted they turn – something tugged at the corners of her memories, but she couldn't quite pull the thought out.

Seamus drove the SUV carefully down the rutted lane, following a stone wall that was overgrown with bramble. The sun struggled to peek through the gray clouds that clung to the horizon, and a lone bird swooped in lazy circles over the road.

If isolation had an image, it would be this place, Sasha thought, as the road stretched ahead of them for ages with nothing in sight but hill after faded green hill. She idly hoped Seamus had filled the car with enough petrol.

"Where are you taking us, girl?" Bianca asked and Sasha shrugged.

"I can't quite say. I just had this overwhelming urge to go up this lane," Sasha admitted, and Declan swore.

"You think it's a trap?" Seamus asked, his eyes meeting Declan's in the rearview mirror.

"I think we should be on full alert," Declan said, sliding a dagger into his hand. Bianca and Maddox both followed suit, arming themselves. Sasha didn't bother – she was in the middle of the car and her gut instinct said it wasn't a trap.

Then again, she'd long ago stopped trusting her instincts, as they clearly hadn't helped her in some situations – like with her ex-fiancé. With that in mind, she gripped the hilt of the dagger and slid it from its hiding place in her boot.

"I see something," Bianca said softly.

A cluster of small, one-room stone huts and a few tents were tucked behind a hill, where there was shelter from the wind that whipped across the land.

"Gypsies," Sasha said, and Bianca turned to nod her agreement.

"This look familiar to you?" Maddox asked, but Sasha just shrugged. She had no way of knowing why she had needed to come this way.

Until she saw the woman step into the road.

"She'll be wanting to talk to me, then," Sasha said, and instructed Seamus to pull the car over. They all went silent and waited.

The woman – easily eighty-five years old if not older, judging from the deep lines that furrowed her face – lifted her chin high and raised one hand to curl her fingers into a beckoning motion. Her clear gray eyes met Sasha's through the windshield.

"I'll go," Sasha said, nudging Maddox to let her out.

"Not without me you won't," Declan said and slipped from the car to stand in front of the woman, hands on his hips.

"Wait," Sasha said, annoyed that he'd barely given her a chance to get out of the car before he spoke with the woman. By the time she reached his side, the woman was chuckling and Declan had relaxed ever so slightly.

"This is Sasha, the one you seek," Declan said, putting his arm around her shoulders and pulling her slightly forward so that his body sheltered hers. Comfort washed through her as his warmth seeped through her from behind. It also reminded her just how much larger this man was than her, as he all but towered over her and protected her from the back.

"I know Sasha. Her eyes are the same, though it has been ages since I've held her," The woman's eyes crinkled at the corners as she smiled gently, running her gaze over Sasha before nodding once in approval. "You've turned out to be an impressive young woman."

"You know me? From when I was a child?" Sasha asked, her eyes searching for any sort of resemblance in the old woman's face. "What is your name?"

"You may call me Clodagh," she said, a smile playing around her lips. "Aye, child, I kept you warm and safe until I could find a home for you."

"Where did I come from? Why didn't you keep me? How long was I with you?" Sasha peppered the woman with questions, and she raised a hand, chuckling.

"First, let's get you in out of this cold. Though our lodgings be humble, you and your friends are welcome here. You'll come to no harm within our borders."

Declan lifted his head and scanned the hills, acknowledging the men he now saw posted at various intervals, as well as the press of magickal wards that safeguarded the place.

"Is she right? Are we safe here?" Sasha asked, turning to look up at him over her shoulder.

He lost his breath for a moment as he looked down into her beautiful eyes. "Aye, we'll be safe here. But we should not tarry long. It's best to keep moving on."

"He's right. But you can take a night. We'll have food, a fire, and you'll be able to camp in our tents. I'm sorry we can't offer more at the time," Clodagh said with a shrug, but Declan waved her away.

"We are a tough breed. There's nothing wrong with tents. We're grateful for your hospitality," Declan said.

Sasha found herself being charmed by his kindness. What was it with this man? She'd successfully ignored dating for several years and now she was all but drooling over this man who spent most of his time deliberately annoying her.

He must have magicked her. Sasha nodded to herself briskly. 'Twas the only explanation.

"How long did you know me for? Did I live here when I was younger?" Sasha asked and Clodagh beamed at her.

"Why don't we get your friends settled and some food on before we have ourselves a wee chat?"

Sasha felt the old familiar angst in the pit of her stomach – the feeling of wondering why she was abandoned, where she really came from, and why no one had wanted her. Shaking it off, she forced herself to push the feeling down. It didn't matter. Not now – not when she had been pulled into a massive quest centuries old, full of magick and fae, and who knows what else. If anything, it was probably selfish to be thinking of herself at a time like this.

"I'm sorry. You're right. This isn't about me. We'd be grateful for a bite and the warmth of the fire," Sasha said easily.

The old woman peered at her through wizened eyes. "It's most certainly about you, little one. And that's just fine for it to be," Clodagh said, her tone almost sharp as she turned and beckoned for the others to follow her.

Sasha mulled that over as they all grabbed their packs from the car and followed the old woman.

The rocky road they were on dipped and twisted, a rutted lane that was worn from footsteps, splitting off like roots from a tree to each hut. Clodagh wound them past the huts, leading them to where tents – the old kind, made of heavy canvas with a wooden floor – were clustered in a row of three.

"It may look like not much, but the canvas is tied tightly, and you'll be warm beneath the wool blankets. You'll be safe here tonight," Clodagh said, gesturing with a hand that was wrinkled with age. Sasha noticed just a bit of a shakiness to it, and wondered briefly just how old Clodagh really was.

"I'm calling this one," Maddox said immediately, and Sasha tilted her head at the wide grin on his face.

"We'll take this one." Bianca gestured to the middle tent, which left the last tent for Sasha and Declan. Sasha slitted her eyes at Maddox, who just shrugged cheerfully.

"I'll stay outside to keep watch," Declan said, and walked away before anyone could respond. Sasha watched him stomp across the field, his head swiveling in all directions as he assessed the land and any weak points of entry.

"Well, that didn't go the way I was hoping," Maddox said.

"Right? What the hell?" Bianca said.

Sasha sighed. "Will you all stop with the matchmaker shite? It's not happening," she said, and stormed into her tent, annoyed with everyone and just wanting to crawl into a bed – any bed – and pull the covers over her head. But that's not what fierce warrior women do, she reminded herself as she slung her pack onto the double cot and assessed her accommodations.

The old woman was correct, Sasha mused, as she crouched and examined where the canvas was connected to the planked floor. With the ceiling coming to a point, a small table with a lantern, and another long table with a jug of water and glasses, the tent was sparse, but cozy. Piled high on the cot were several pillows and decidedly lovely woven blankets that immediately provided Sasha with a feeling of comfort. She wondered if magick had been woven into them.

She paused. She'd barely believed in magick days ago,

and now here she was seeing spells and magicks woven into blankets? Sasha reminded herself that a true master always remained open to learning. If she was to conquer this mission that had been handed to her, well, she'd need to suspend all disbelief and keep her mind open.

It just might save her life.

# CHAPTER 19

"Well, it's not exactly glamping, is it?" Maddox said as he zipped his leather coat tightly and sniffed once for emphasis.

"Glamping?" Sasha raised an eyebrow at him.

"Glamourous camping," Bianca said, leaning around Maddox to look at Sasha. "It's like where all the rich people want to go camping and do outdoorsy stuff but want all the fancy accommodations of a hotel."

"Why is this even a thing?" Sasha wondered. "If you're going camping, don't you want to camp?"

"They sing songs by the fire and muck around in the hills, but still have fancy food and designer sheets," Bianca continued.

"Why would you pay to go hiking?" Sasha asked, sweeping her hand out to gesture at the hills behind them, where the last of the day's light was just peeking over the tops. "There's hills and hikes everywhere. It's free to go for a nice walk."

"Speaking of a nice walk…" Maddox murmured and

Sasha turned to see Declan striding across the hill, his shoulders back, his hair tucked beneath a woolen cap. He looked every inch the master of his domain – and it didn't seem to matter what the domain was. If he was in it, he owned it.

"Aye, he's a fine one, isn't he?" Clodagh asked cheerfully from behind them, and Sasha almost bit her tongue to stop herself from biting out a nasty retort. It was becoming increasingly annoying how much Declan was intruding upon her thoughts.

"Clodagh, I meant to ask, is there a bathroom we can make use of?" Sasha asked, deliberately turning her back on Declan.

"Aye, there's a bathroom and shower house just around this way." Clodagh pointed it out and Sasha nodded her thanks. "Come meet us by the fire shortly. We've got a nice lamb stew simmering and a wee bit of whiskey to share. It will be enough to warm your bellies."

They all made use of the sparsely appointed bathhouse and returned to wander toward the fire. Several people were clustered around it, many wrapped in long cloaks, all busy attending to one task or the other. Sasha felt oddly out of place with nothing to do, so she immediately approached Clodagh and offered her help.

"Sit, sit. You are honored guests," Clodagh said, gesturing to one of the long benches tucked by the fire. "We give thanks to our Goddess by providing our hospitality to you as well as a bit of wee help along the journey."

Sasha tilted her head in question at Clodagh. "You know what we're about then, do you?"

"Aye, child, I know."

"Can you tell us where the sword is?" Sasha demanded and Clodagh threw her head back and laughed, taking easily twenty years off her face. Sasha could see that she had once been a great beauty.

"I'm fairly certain you're the only one who can be telling us that," Clodagh said, and Sasha went to sit on the bench, crossing her arms over her chest and finding herself inexplicably grumpy.

Why was she the one who was supposed to have all the answers? She had just learned of this stupid legend. Everyone else had known about it for ages and they could've spent at least some time researching it. Now it was all on her to figure out?

"What's with the face?" Declan demanded and Sasha started, turning to look up at where he stood by the fire.

"Do you need to be sneaking up on me, then?" Sasha demanded.

A quick grin flashed in Declan's face, making Sasha's heart skip as the light from the flames played on the angles of his cheekbones.

"I hardly crept. You were lost in thought and clearly having a bit of wallow."

"Excuse me? I was not wallowing," Sasha said, glaring at Declan. Had she been wallowing?

"I know a grumpy face when I see one," Declan said, his eyes leveled on hers.

"I'm not grumpy," Sasha said, but even as she said it she realized how grumpy she sounded. "Fine, whatever. I'm annoyed. It's not your problem."

"Everything with you is my problem. Talk," Declan

demanded, sitting down next to her on the bench. His nearness made Sasha's body jolt to attention.

"Gee, that's a surefire way to get someone to spill their
secrets to you – call them a problem and then demand they
talk," Sasha said, her grumpiness growing. She tried to
edge slightly away from him, conscious of how big his
body was next to hers and how her body seemed to tingle
anywhere they touched.

Declan sighed and scratched his head briefly, adjusting
the wool cap, before stretching his long legs out in front of
him so that his feet almost reached the fire.

"Sasha, tell me what is bothering you," he said, his
voice rumbling against her as he closed the gap she had
just created between them.

"I'm just annoyed that I have to be the one to figure
everything out when all of you have been privy to this
knowledge for ages. Like, couldn't you have done some
research? Gathered a few clues? Something? If you knew
you were going on this epic quest, one would think you'd
be a little more prepared. Instead you're letting the least
prepared, and the least-educated in anything fae, to be the
merry little leader of this ragtag group we've got here."

"Anything else?" Declan asked dryly.

Sasha wanted to smack him on the leg, but refrained
from doing so. "Why are you sleeping outside tonight?"
she demanded and then almost slapped a hand over her
face. Where had that come from?

"Are you worried you'll be lonely, then?" Declan said,
his eyes dancing with delight at her question.

Sasha buried her face in her hands, all pride lost in the
moment. "I just think it's ridiculous that you take this aloof

stance from all of us. You can keep warm in a tent is all," Sasha grumbled.

"It's my job to protect you. How am I going to do that if I don't keep watch?"

"You're safe here," Clodagh said, overhearing his comment as she came forward offering two bowls of stew. Sasha almost groaned in delight at the sight of thick chunks of potatoes and carrots swimming in a thick broth in a cheerful blue earthenware bowl. Smiling, she took the bowl and immediately dipped her spoon in.

"I agree." Declan inclined his head in thanks as he took the bowl from Clodagh, the bowl almost disappearing in his large hands. "Your wards are excellent and I can feel the stronghold you've created. Excellent magick. I don't suspect we'll have trouble tonight. Still."

"Your only job tonight is to be what you need to be," Clodagh admonished him lightly.

Sasha wondered just what that meant, but was distracted by Bianca sitting next to her.

"This stew is amazing," Bianca exclaimed and immediately peppered Clodagh with questions for the secret ingredients. Silence fell around them as the group dug into their dinner, and Sasha let her eyes wander over everyone seated around the fire. There were several men, but more women, and only a few children. The family resemblance was striking, and Sasha wondered how long they'd lived here. Might any of them recognize her?

"You're wondering about how you know us, aren't you?" Clodagh asked, and her eyes, gleaming across the fire at Sasha, seemed young in contrast to her wizened face.

"I don't really have a history," Sasha shrugged. "It's natural to wonder where I came from."

The family remained silent, and it was clear that Clodagh was going to lead this conversation, though one woman did nod at Sasha across the fire.

"Aye, 'tis natural," Clodagh agreed, brandishing a bottle of whiskey and distributing it among small cups.

The wind picked up, teasing Sasha's braid and sending a chill down her back. She stiffened when Declan put his arm loosely around her waist, drawing her in just slightly for warmth. She shouldn't allow this, Sasha admonished herself, but his nearness felt nice.

Like he fit.

"It was a night much like this one, but colder, you understand? The damp was the kind that seeps into the bones, and most of us were huddled up and in for the night. Except for me. I'd had an anxiousness that day – something that kept me pacing. 'Tis rare that feeling comes for me, as we are wanderers and we take the days as they come. Living in the present allows us to pay little attention to anxiety or happy or unhappy; we just are, you understand me? There's no need or want for this deep existential study of happiness. We exist."

Sasha nodded. It was pragmatism at its best, and something she could certainly get on board with.

"Yet that day, I was restless. I decided to wander that night, leaving the safety of our circle and walking into the night. I closed my eyes and listened, lifted my face to the wind, and read the energy of the earth. Nothing was amiss. Now, my magick is not fae magick and not any magick that you need to fully understand, but I trust my instincts and what I've learned through the years. The natural world was giving me no concerns. And yet the anxiety persisted. I continued walking." Clodagh gestured with her hand toward the hills. "And then I saw it."

"Saw what?" Sasha asked.

"Light flickering. As though someone had a fire burning, much like this one, way up on the hills. I didn't hesitate to investigate, although thinking back, 'twas foolish of me to go alone. I worry little about mortal dangers though." Clodagh shrugged as though that attitude were normal, and Sasha wondered once again just what type of magick hers was.

"What happened next?" Bianca asked, scraping the bottom of her soup bowl.

"I found the light – and I was correct, it was a fire. But like none I have ever seen, before or since. It was most certainly magick," Clodagh said, turning a sharp eye on Sasha. "It was a lovely bluish-white, almost like the deepest point of a flame, you understand? And it was a circle. Within the circle was – well, was *you*, my child."

"I was in a fire?" Sasha exclaimed.

"Aye, though the fire didn't touch you. I sensed it was more for protection. And you looked up at me, calm as could be, and waited for me to pick you up. I reached right through the flames, not feeling an ounce of pain – which was how I knew I was meant to be the one finding you – and took you into my arms. I brought you back with me, knowing that you were touched, but unsure of what that meant."

"Isn't there some American song like that?" Bianca demanded.

Sasha turned to look at her. "Shut up. 'Ring of Fire'?" she said, feeling the beginnings of a hysterical bubble rising in her throat.

"Yes! A country-western one!" Bianca hummed a few notes and despite herself, Sasha found herself humming along. It was a catchy tune.

"Except instead of falling into the fire, you were pulled from it," Maddox said, smiling at Sasha.

"Was there anything with her?" Declan interrupted the levity, his deep voice rumbling in his chest against Sasha's side.

"Aye, there was. The instructions said to give it to her when the time was right. I've never opened it."

"Oh! A clue!" Bianca clapped her hands in delight and Seamus squeezed her shoulder. Sasha found herself oddly comforted at having them along on this journey now. Bianca's joy and wide-eyed delight in all things fae brought an innocent yearning to the quest that made Sasha more intrigued. She found herself hungering for more information – much as the rest of them were.

"Clare had a clue too, from her parents. It was this beautiful ring. I wonder if you'll get a piece of jewelry too. Like 'one ring to bind them all,'" Bianca said, her pretty face squinched in thought.

"Personal talismans are powerful," Declan murmured.

Sasha had to wonder what else she could need. She already had a dagger that could shoot fire.

"I want to hear what happened next. Why didn't I stay with you?" Sasha waved away the clue and focused on Clodagh. A part of her thought her life would have been significantly better if she'd been allowed to stay with these magickal wandering gypsy-folk instead of being thrust into the arms of unwilling foster parents.

"We couldn't protect you at the time, my child. I gladly would have kept you. Och, you were the happiest baby," Clodagh said, a smile creasing her face in remembrance. "Those big eyes, and laughing at everything."

"I don't remember being a cheerful child," Sasha said stiffly, feeling uncomfortable at the thought of having been a happy baby. Frankly, she couldn't remember her childhood being happy at all.

"You were. You radiated light. I'm sorry you lost that," Clodagh said, and Sasha stiffened, her guard up. This was dangerously close to discussing things she didn't like to recall.

"It's fine. You took me out of here then? To Kilkenny?" Sasha prodded, wanting to move past the images of her as a laughing baby.

"Aye, to a family in Kilkenny. The house was warded and it was understood that lookouts in the city would assist if needed – which was more than we could offer. Though my heart did pinch a bit having to let you go. It's good to see you, though I barely can reconcile the baby that once was with this fierce warrior woman in front of me." Clodagh appraised her with eyes that Sasha thought saw way too clearly. "That lightness is still in you, child."

"Light and laughter can get you killed, it appears." Sasha shrugged her comment away.

"Light and laughter is what we fight for," Declan said softly and Sasha found herself feeling oddly betrayed.

"What are you trying to say? That I'm ruining the

mission?" Sasha asked, turning to move out from under his arm, which no longer felt very protecting.

"I'm saying that darkness will always be there. We fight for the light. That's the way of things. You can shrug it off or stuff it away or whatever you're doing – but we've all known pain and loss. You have to look for the light. In the everyday, in the hardest moments, in the darkest of paths – you must find the light. It is, quite simply, the only reason to keep forging ahead."

Sasha's pulse picked up as his words seemed to chip away at the pit of anxiety in her stomach, making her clench both fists, her nails digging deeply into her palms.

"What do you know of loss, Declan? What do you know of sadness? You're living out what apparently is the highest honor of your people. You can't possibly know what it is to drop from nowhere and have to forge your own way. Always being the odd one out, never fully fitting in," Sasha all but spat out, her eyes leveled on Declan's.

"Can't I?" Declan said softly, his eyes holding hers. "I've been a Protector for ages. This role meant I left my family, my future, everything so I could honor the Goddess by protecting you on this most sacred of quests. How is that not loss? How is that not loneliness? And yet I look for the light. Every day. And I see it in you, especially when you are unguarded, when your walls are down. When I catch you laughing at something silly when nobody is watching and your face glows from within. Aye, the light is there. You've but to let it out."

"I didn't realize I was going to be psychoanalyzed tonight," Sasha said stiffly, rising and nodding to Clodagh. "I'm for bed. Thank you kindly for dinner."

"But what about the clue?" Bianca's voice trailed off as Sasha stalked into the darkness, her stomach rolling in angst and unhappiness. Why couldn't anyone understand that she didn't want this role?

All she wanted was to be left alone.

# CHAPTER 20

"**Y**ou can't just run away every time something scares you," Declan growled from behind her.

Sasha whirled, almost stumbling when she bumped against his chest. "Excuse me? Who said I was scared?" Sasha demanded, slamming her fist into his chest to try and get him to step back. It was like hitting stone.

"It's obvious you are. Warriors aren't supposed to retreat when things get uncomfortable," Declan said, his face unreadable as he watched her.

"What makes you think you can talk to me this way? Just because you've stalked me for years doesn't mean you know me," Sasha hissed, jamming her finger into his chest now as her temper heated.

"Stalked you?! I protected you. You'd have been dead long ago if it weren't for me," Declan sneered, his honor offended.

"I protect myself, buddy. Nobody else has. Where were

you with all the fae I've been killing for months? Some Protector," Sasha scoffed.

Storm clouds washed over Declan's face. "Oh? Did you think there was just one at a time coming after you, then? While you killed one, I was busy with the twenty behind him. It seems you think you know everything, princess, when you've barely scratched the surface. I'd advise you to get your head out of your arse and start confronting things head-on."

"I do confront things head-on," Sasha hissed, temper making her blood heat. "I just don't see how we need to dissect my childhood. It has nothing to do with the quest."

"Doesn't it? Everything matters. It's all part and parcel of it. You need to realize that this has been a journey in the making. You can't leave any stone unturned. Even if that means examining things that make you uncomfortable."

Sasha hated how reasonable he sounded. But what did he know? Sure, he had to leave family behind, but they'd probably all had good relationships and he could talk to them whenever. It was far different than having grown up like she had.

"Let's see what makes you uncomfortable, then," Sasha said, surprising herself before she stopped thinking altogether and reached up to press her lips to his.

For one moment, stillness hung in the air as neither moved, their lips pressed together, energy coursing between them.

Declan broke the kiss before it became more heated between them and cursed before turning on his heel and striding into the darkness.

"Who's retreating now?" Sasha called, delighted with

having the last word, though her insides burned with a heat she couldn't quite tamp down.

Talk about running away from things that made you uncomfortable, Sasha thought, and pulled back the flap to her tent feeling oddly comforted. Maybe she'd sleep tonight after all.

# CHAPTER 21

*S*he should have known sleep wouldn't come easy. Still, she'd expected more than the few hours she finally did get – after lying awake doing her best not to think about the one thing her body seemed to want her to think about.

Declan's touch. His nearness. His everything. Being around him seemed to scatter her brain and she decidedly disliked it. If she was distracted, someone could die.

Sasha sighed and pushed herself up from the cot, wondering where Declan had slept, or if he had slept at all. She knew she should apologize to Clodagh. The woman had saved her, for goodness sake, and here she had a fit? She scrubbed her eyes as she groggily crossed the tent and pushed the flap back.

Was she still dreaming?

The huts were gone, as was the fire pit. The only thing that remained were the three tents clustered together and the car. Sasha scratched her head and wondered what kind of weird fae magick this was. Perhaps she'd dreamed the entire episode?

Until Bianca poked her head out of her own tent and gasped.

"So it's not just me then?" Sasha asked, rubbing a palm across her sleepy eyes.

"How could they have disappeared so quickly? There isn't even a spot where the fire was!" Bianca pulled her head back into the tent and called to Seamus. "Seamus, Clodagh is gone. Are you sure you don't know what kind of magick she is made of?"

Seamus poked his head out of the tent and looked around, his red hair sticking up in all directions, giving Sasha a pretty good idea of what they'd been doing the night before.

"I'm not sure what magick she was, but she certainly had strong wards protecting this place. I wonder why they left," Seamus said.

"I'm sure it was because of me," Sasha said, and looked them both in the eyes. "I'm sorry for that. I should've come back out by the fire and set things right."

"Clodagh didn't seem overly fussed about it. I think we all know the incredible amount of stress on your shoulders." Seamus shrugged, and Bianca nodded her agreement.

"Is that the clue then? The package by your foot?" Bianca pointed to a small package that lay at the front of Sasha's tent, something she had missed entirely. She wondered what else she'd missed, and scanned the horizon, seeking anything amiss, before bending over to retrieve the package.

"Why do you think it's a clue? What if it's just a gift?" Sasha wondered, tugging at the twine that wrapped the package.

"Wait – don't you want Declan here to open it with you?"

"What does Declan have to do with this?" Sasha wondered.

"I'm a part of this whether you like it or not," Declan said, stepping around the corner of the tent. Sasha could've stamped her foot in frustration. The man had serious skills when it came to sneaking around.

"I just meant that I don't know what you'd have to do with a gift that was left for me," Sasha said, feeling annoyed by his nearness. The man made her itchy.

"Destiny is destiny," Declan said, raising an eyebrow at her.

It was all Sasha could do not to roll her eyes. She was beginning to get distinctly annoyed with the concept that her life had been preordained for her and everything she'd been working toward was irrelevant.

"So that's it then? You'll just blindly do what the Goddess says – follow me everywhere through life because of destiny? What about free will? What do you want with your life?" Sasha asked, her finger pulling at the twine as she faced him.

"I want what is best for you," Declan said, his eyes serious.

"But what about your needs and wants?"

"My needs are met if your wants are met."

"You aren't some spineless blob, though," Sasha argued, for some reason feeling the need to stick on this point. "You must have dreams or wants outside of this... job of yours."

"I do. But those are for after. For now, I'm solely concerned with your safety and happiness."

"See how he said 'her happiness,' too. That's not required of a Protector," Bianca said to Seamus, poking him in the ribs with her elbow, a delighted smile on her face.

"Oh, would you stop looking for something that isn't there?" Sasha grumbled, but Bianca only chuckled.

"Isn't it, though?" Declan asked.

Sasha paused for a moment as her eyes met his.

"Ohhhhhhh," Bianca breathed, and Seamus nudged her to be quiet.

"You didn't seem so interested last night," Sasha spat, her hands at her hips now as she leveled a look at him.

"Last night? What happened last night?" Bianca said in a stage whisper, and Seamus shushed her again. Maddox stepped from his tent but stopped immediately as he noticed the missing huts and the stand-off between Declan and Sasha.

"It has nothing to do with whether I am interested or not," Declan said, the tenor of his voice seeming to hum with a sexuality that warmed Sasha's very insides.

"Then what, pray tell, does it have to do with?" Sasha demanded.

"I'm a warrior on a mission. The mission comes first. Sex with you would be a distraction," Declan said with ease, almost as if he was speaking to a child. Don't throw petrol on the fire, small one, you see? It only causes an explosion.

"I don't recall offering sex," Sasha said, narrowing her eyes at Declan.

He shrugged one ridiculously broad shoulder and looked off to the horizon for a moment before pinning her with his gaze again.

"It was understood."

"A kiss doesn't mean sex. I don't know what century you're from, but that kind of assumption can land you in jail," Sasha argued, feeling a flush of embarrassment wash through her as her friends listened in rapt attention.

A flash of anger crossed Declan's devastatingly handsome face, and he stepped forward until he stood but inches away, towering over her. She'd clearly offended his honor.

"I would never take what you weren't offering," Declan bit out, his eyes never leaving hers. "But it is understood that we will be together. I will decide the time and the place – and I will not allow it to distract from the mission. But understand this, Sasha Flanagan. You are meant for me."

A sliver of light bloomed in Sasha's chest, even as the spark of anger lit in her gut. The conflicting emotions of excitement and frustration at being told what would happen with her future made her want to stamp her foot like a child having a tantrum.

Declan left her no chance to respond. In nothing more than half a second, he'd disappeared, moving at his preternatural speed, and Sasha let out a breath she hadn't realized she'd been holding in.

"Darling, that man is deliciousness on a stick. I'd just

lap him up the first second you get," Maddox declared, fanning his face dramatically.

Bianca laughed in agreement. "This is awesome. You guys are stunning together."

"There is no 'together.' It's not happening. He doesn't get to order me around like that," Sasha said, her words like a bucket of ice over her friends' excitement.

"Methinks you don't have much of a say in it," Maddox said, and Sasha glared at him.

"Can we just open this gift and move on? There is no time for such nonsense." Sasha tore at the twine, distinctly annoyed at Declan for having said those things in front of everyone. Meant for him? Please. The nerve of that man.

They barely knew each other.

Fiercely shoving those thoughts away, she unwrapped the package to find a small wooden box with a quaternary knot – mirroring the one on her scalp – intricately carved into the lid. The age of the box was evident to Sasha and she handled it gently as she lifted the lid to reveal a necklace snuggled gently against lush black velvet.

"Oh, I'm dying over here. What is it?" Bianca exclaimed, all but wringing her hands in excitement.

"It's a pendant. Cat's-eye, probably eighteenth-century judging from the metalwork here," Sasha said, holding the necklace up so that the stone gleamed in the early morning sunshine, the light of the cat's-eye flashing almost white.

"What an unusual choice for a stone," Bianca mused, coming over to trace a finger gently over the pendant. Sasha almost jerked it back, surprised to find how protective she felt of the stone. That odd reaction was something to note, she thought to herself as she allowed Bianca to examine it.

"Cat's-eye is known to help with building your intuition, aiding you in trusting your instincts, and helping you let go of the past," Bianca continued. "But I also wonder if there is something to do with the light. See how the light catches it? The other clue had something to do with light as well. And we are looking for the Sword of Light, or Sword of Truth, depending on which legends you subscribe to. All in all, I'd say this is a very intriguing stone to be used."

"There's a bit of paper in the box," Sasha said, tugging the corner of the velvet to reveal a small scroll, tied with a red ribbon and yellowed with age.

*Your mind's eye knows the truth.*

"Hmm. The first talked about knowing the dark to know the light, and this one is about trusting your instincts," Bianca mused.

Sasha turned to look at her. "That's the second time you've said to trust my instincts."

"It is?" Bianca shrugged. "I'm just rambling. Speaking what pops in my head."

But it was more than that. Sasha felt it to her very core as she scanned the empty landscape in front of them.

"We need to move. And now."

The ambush began before the words were out of her mouth.

# CHAPTER 22

They reacted instantly, and the swiftness of their response surprised Sasha, Maddox's most of all. She'd only known him in the capacity of outrageous gay best friend – not as a magick-wielding fae warrior.

"I thought we were safe here," Sasha shouted as she ran to stand back-to-back with her friends, the dagger raised in front of her chest.

"The protection left with Clodagh," Seamus said as they pirouetted, waiting for the first of the Domnua that had snuck over the hills to make their move.

"I'd put that necklace on," Bianca suggested, and Sasha realized with a surprise that it was still dangling from her hand.

Slipping it over her neck, she felt it warm against her skin as it slid beneath her shirt, the pendant nestling just above her heart.

Where was Declan? Would they be able to warn him without alerting the Domnua? Sasha's gaze darted right and left as she struggled to catch a glimpse of him. The hills were silent so early in the morning. Not even a bird bothered to sing its morning song, as if even they knew that the magick sneaking across those hills was dangerous.

"Now!" Maddox exclaimed as the Domnua exploded into a frenzy at once, their silver glow only betraying their movements slightly as they surged in a wave of impending doom toward where Sasha and the others stood.

Sasha lashed out with her dagger, the training as instinctive to her as her next breath, dipping and slashing as she worked her way through Domnua after Domnua, their silvery blood splashing across her before disappearing in a flash of magick. She barely caught a flash of Bianca, a rounded whirling dervish doing the same, and found herself almost laughing at her stalwart fierceness. It was a reminder to not let a perky face and guileless blue eyes mislead her.

"Finally, we'll take you. Just like we took your parents. Just wait until you watch them being tortured." A Domnua danced in front of her, his face wreathed in delight as he swung a dagger back and forth.

"What? My parents? Where?" Sasha demanded, her eyes tracking the fae's every movement.

"Your favorite place." The Domnua grinned right before Seamus's dagger sliced through his throat, causing him to disappear in a splatter of silver. Sasha gaped down at the puddle, trying to understand what the fae had said.

A Domnua's blade almost slipped past her guard as Sasha was distracted by a movement up on the ridge – Declan, his shout loud and clear in the morning quiet – which made the Domnua turn as one and look at him.

"I have the sword, not her," Declan shouted again and

Sasha's stomach flipped over as the entire group of Domnua, fifty or so of them, turned at once and raced for where Declan stood, his shoulders back, his sword at the ready.

"Now might be a good time to try out that nifty fireball thing you've got going on," Bianca said.

Sasha would have slapped herself in the forehead if she wasn't holding a deadly weapon. "On it," she said, shaking her head a bit in disbelief that she'd forgotten, then leveling the dagger at the crowd of Domnua and working to summon the anger deep within her core. She allowed the fire to swirl, creeping its way up before it shot its way from the dagger, a blinding flash of heat that leveled the Domnua in one fell swoop. Declan stood there, his sword still at the ready, his head swiveling as he looked for any last Domnua. Finding none, he inclined his head in a nod toward Sasha before disappearing over the ridge. Presumably to kill more Domnua, or to lick his wounded pride after Sasha had saved him.

"I just love all the flash-bang dramatics you Seekers get," Bianca gushed, throwing her arm around Sasha's shoulders for a quick squeeze before squealing when Seamus swept her up for a kiss. "Seamus, stop, you'll drop me. I'm too heavy."

"You're light as a feather, my love, and pretty as roses," Seamus said, his face alight with love as he planted a heavy kiss on Bianca. Sasha smiled, but turned away to search the horizon for Declan once again.

"He's fine," Maddox said, coming to stand at her side and working at a spot of silver that still clung to his shirt.

"I know. I'm just looking for any other Domnua," Sasha said in irritation.

"Lie to him all you want, honey, but you can't lie to me. You've got a thing for that man – and for that, I do not blame you. If he played for my team, I'd be all over him myself."

"Enough of that. We need to go. My parents are in trouble."

If only Sasha could figure out what her favorite place was.

# CHAPTER 23

*D*eclan paced the hill, looking for any warning – any sign of lingering Domnua – but none came. Instead, the sun struggled to peek through the clouds and the birds had begun to sing their morning song, which told Declan that the magick had left the region for now.

It had been nothing but a search party – to test their strength. And here Sasha had leveled them all instead of allowing Declan to do what he'd trained his whole life to do. He swore and kicked at a loose rock on the ground, sending it tumbling down the side of the hill.

Not that she hadn't looked every inch the fierce warrior as she'd done so, Declan thought, feeling a small clutch in his chest as pride swelled. His fierce pint-sized warrior coming into her own. She had a ways to go before she realized just what she was capable of – and he planned to be by her every step of the way as she did, Declan thought with a smile. She was, quite simply, magnificent.

A thought slipped through his head about her determination to pretend they weren't meant for each other. He scoffed and looked off at the horizon. He could feel the current of energy that ran between them when they touched. It was everything he could do not to throw her over his shoulder and take her away – anywhere but here. He wanted to spend days – no, weeks – showing her just how right they would be together.

Not yet. Declan promised himself he would retain his decorum and his promise until the sword was found. But after that? All bets were off.

And Sasha Flanagan would realize they were meant for each other.

He glanced up as the car crested the hill, Seamus at the wheel. Bianca rolled the window down and hung her head out, two blonde pigtails bouncing in the wind. Declan almost grinned at how much like a pert schoolgirl she looked.

"Not to interrupt your sulk or anything, but we've got to move," Bianca said.

Declan found himself almost laughing as a wide grin split his face. "I'm most certainly not sulking. I was just making sure there was nothing else over the hill for us to battle. Let's go," he said. He climbed into the back of the car, where Sasha still sat in the middle seat, her nose as high in the air as it could get.

"Nice shooting, beautiful," Declan said easily.

Sasha jerked to look at him in surprise. "I thought you'd be angry," she exclaimed.

"Why? We're all on the same team here. I love watching a woman own her power," Declan said, allowing the double meaning to hang in the air. Sasha looked away, but a faint tinge of pink clung to her cheeks. Declan bit back a smile as he imagined that same color heating her face when he finally took her to bed.

"Oh my," Maddox whispered, fanning his face, and Bianca burst out in laughter.

# CHAPTER 24

*H*ere she'd thought he would be mad that she'd gone and stolen his thunder, but instead he'd complimented her. The man remained an enigma to Sasha, and one that she found herself increasingly interested in figuring out. It seemed she needed to suspend some of her long-held assumptions about most men in her life, and instead sit back and study him.

"Honey, tell us what the Domnua said again." Maddox patted her thigh gently, bringing Sasha back into the moment.

"Basically he said they have my parents – and in my favorite place. I'm not sure what or where that is, though," Sasha said, feeling a sense of helplessness seep through her. It could be anywhere, really. Or from what time in her life?

"Well, if it's your parents, perhaps it was from when you were growing up? Like, did you have a favorite place as a child? Or someplace that always made you happy?"

"The Nest," Sasha said automatically, then paused.

"The Nest?" Bianca looked over her head in question.

"It's just this darling little tea shop-pub-bookstore type place. It has mismatched furniture, and sort of a relaxed everyone-is-welcome type of vibe. I always liked going there and reading a book in the corner. In all honesty, it felt more like home than home did." Sasha shrugged that last comment away, but Maddox patted her leg gently.

"To The Nest we go then," Bianca said.

"Why do you think they went after my parents? I mean, they aren't really my parents. Not by blood. Not anything that would be linked to this quest, is what I mean," Sasha shrugged, running her finger over the pendant at her neck, feeling the smooth contours of the stone.

"There must be a link there or something that you have to overcome," Bianca suggested. "Typically in a quest, there are three hurdles you have to pass in order to get to the treasure. Maybe this is the first?"

"And that little showing of Domnua wasn't?" Sasha asked. "And why did Clodagh disappear?"

"She gave you your pendant. It's part of your power. Her job was done. She was smart to clear out and protect her family. This is a war. As a leader of a clan, I would have done the same," Declan said.

Sasha looked at him in surprise. "Basically deliver the package, task complete, clear out?"

"Her purpose was served. It would be foolhardy to stay and put her family in harm."

"But–" Sasha bit off her words. A part of her thought she was Clodagh's family – and wasn't that just a kick in the pants?

"You thought of her as family?" Declan asked softly.

Sasha saw a look of sympathy cross Bianca's face, which immediately made her put her walls up. "No, I just thought she'd feel a bit of responsibility for me as she was the one who saved my life as a babe. No matter, though. She did her job, I have my pendant, and we have a clue as to where to go next." Sasha shrugged it away and saw Bianca press her lips together to hold back whatever she had been about to say.

"Are you worried about your parents? When is the last time you spoke to them?" Seamus asked instead, and Sasha turned to the task at hand.

"It's been quite a while. I didn't really feel like I fit in all that well with the family." Sasha shrugged again, uncomfortable with bringing up family stuff.

"Yeah, but you can not fit in and they still love you," Bianca pointed out. "Do you not feel that's the case?"

"As I said before, I feel like the love is conditional. If I fit in and do the right things, then I'm loved. If I go my own way and live an oddball life, then maybe not so much," Sasha said, biting her lip as she stared out the window.

"But how is running your own business and being a successful antiques dealer an 'oddball life'?" Bianca asked.

"I think it's just because I'm a strong woman and they don't necessarily understand me. I don't have a craving to have children and be a stay-at-home mum, so I've fallen outside the norm of what they understand. I'm not even certain it's malicious. I'm just not sure that they'll ever accept me for who I am."

Silence filled the car at her words, as there was really nothing much else that could be said. Some things were the untenable truth and there was no sugarcoating it. It wasn't bad or good – it simply was.

"We'll find out soon enough why we're being sent on this path. Rest your head for now," Declan said, putting his arm around Sasha and pulling her tight against him, though she kept her arms crossed and shoulders stiff.

It took her less than a minute to drift off.

# CHAPTER 25

*S*asha awoke with a start, surprised to find herself snuggled into the crook of Declan's arm, her hand resting on the washboard muscles of his stomach. Dear lord, this is not how you keep your cool, she thought, as she slowly extricated herself from his grip without making eye contact with him.

They'd entered a small village near the town where Sasha had grown up. She remembered furiously pedaling her bike to the village each day – anything to get out of town and away to something new, where she could be herself without the questioning eyes of her family.

Sasha pressed her eyes closed against the memories that swamped her as they wound their way through the colorful downtown of the teeny village. The old feelings of insecurity that had made her stick her head in a book in the corner of The Nest day after day, the feeling of anger that nobody seemed to understand her, her frustration at having no control over her life other than being able to bike to the next village. She remembered reading books on swordplay and antique weapons until the pages were falling out. Having found a manual on fencing, she'd begun her first cautious steps into the martial arts with a thin branch that she'd poke and parry behind the stone walls of the pastures lining the village roads.

She'd been the oddball in her family and in school. She was the smallest in her level so she was never picked for sports, and the quiet one in class who scored well on exams. It had been a fairly solitary existence growing up, and she'd longed for more friends, perhaps even a boyfriend. It wasn't until she finally went out on her own that she promised she would shed that skin and come into her own. Sasha had worked diligently through the years to escape the awkwardness and insecurity of her youth, and felt like she'd done a good job of coming into her own.

Up until Aaron had cheated on her, anyway. It had been more of a blow to her confidence than she'd expected. Though she'd picked up and carried on, Sasha had seriously struggled with trusting her instincts – in fact, with trusting anyone – for a while after.

She paused for a moment. Hadn't Bianca brought up trusting her instincts twice earlier today? It was something to mull over. If anything, her job was to identify patterns or tug on any threads that seemed to be woven together in this fantastical quest she found herself on. She decided to shelve that thought for later, though, as Seamus turned down the street that held The Nest.

"This is charming," Bianca murmured.

Sasha found a smile creeping across her face. It was eclectic, and warm, and one of the few places that truly brought warm memories for her. Tucked along a small side street, The Nest was a charming gray stone building with mismatched windows – some oval-shaped, some large and paned, others tiny diamond-shaped stained glass. Little pots that would hold flowers in the summer, statues of gnomes and fairies, and other odds and ends lined the walkway and wall of the garden behind it.

"It's one of my favorite spots. It's quite cozy inside, especially in the winter with the fire going. You can tuck yourself away in a corner with a book and relax for hours," Sasha murmured, but her eyes were scanning the empty street. She noticed that Declan was doing the same.

"Is it usually this empty?" Seamus asked, and Sasha shook her head, her hand tightening around the hilt of her dagger.

"They want us to come here. But why even give us a heads up that this is a trap? I don't understand," Bianca asked.

"I don't know. The fae are a tricky lot. There's always more than meets the eye," Declan said, and both Seamus and Maddox nodded in agreement.

"I'll remember that," Sasha said, her tone stiff as she ran her eyes over Declan for a second.

Seamus pulled up next to the building and let the car idle as they waited to make a decision on what they should do next. Tom Petty's "Free Falling" played low through the speakers and Sasha felt like she could identify with that – it was as though she had fallen into an alternate universe. For the first time, she identified with Alice in Wonderland.

"I'm going in," Sasha decided. She nudged Maddox to move, since she was certain Declan wouldn't let her out.

"Wait a minute. If you go in – we all go in," Bianca declared, and Seamus nodded his head.

"Sorry, sparky, but you don't get to be all warrior badass on your own. We're a team," Seamus said.

Sasha rolled her eyes in annoyance. "Fine, whatever. But they clearly brought us here for a reason, and we aren't going to figure out what that reason is if we just sit in the car. So we might as well just get to it."

"Impatient, are we?" Maddox murmured.

"I feel like a sitting duck in this car. At least if we are out we can move around," Sasha said, anxiety skittering through her stomach. It was more than that, though. She knew her foster parents were inside and she wasn't certain what condition she was going to find them in – or if she was fully prepared to deal with the emotions that would come with whatever she did find.

"If the lady wants to get it over with, then we get it over with. Look alive, everyone. Don't forget to look up either. Those buggers like to be sneaky," Seamus said cheerfully, and everyone moved to leave the car. Sasha was about to exit on Maddox's side when Declan snagged her arm and dragged her unceremoniously with him, much to her chagrin.

"You don't need to tug me around like I'm a small child," Sasha snapped as he kept her close as they rounded the car.

"It's easier than arguing with you," Declan said simply, shielding her with his body as they walked toward the front door. The stillness of the street made Sasha's neck shiver and she continued to scan their surroundings, looking for anything that struck her as out of the ordinary, besides the silence.

"I should go in first..." Sasha's voice trailed off, because Seamus had already opened the door. He poked his head in and then looked back at them, a look of confusion on his face.

"It's oddly normal in here. But I can feel the magick," Seamus murmured and they all crowded around him to peek into the door.

It was just as Sasha had remembered it – warm, with several people reading or drinking a pint around the open room while a lilting Celtic melody hung suspended in the air. She quickly spotted her parents in the corner, smiling and looking relaxed.

Which immediately put her even more on guard. Her parents had rarely been relaxed when she was with them. They were either angry, tense, or worried about money. The only joy she'd really seen in them was when they conversed with their daughter – their real daughter, that is. She'd often tried to understand why they'd even taken her in if they hadn't wanted another daughter.

Her mum, blonde curls tumbling over her back, laughed at something her dad said and sipped from her tea. Her father, also blond, with a thick beard that made him look like a bewildered lion, smiled back at her. For a moment, the years fell away and they seemed to look just like a young couple enjoying themselves. Sasha's heart tugged a bit as she framed them in a new light – as just people living their lives and dealing with the day-to-day as best they knew how.

"Can they see us?" Bianca asked, and Sasha realized

that nobody in the room had turned to look at the open door.

"No. I think we are walking into a staged scene. Arm yourselves. Let's accomplish whatever we need to accomplish here and get out," Declan growled in her ear, the tension all but vibrating off of him and through Sasha as she pressed herself to him.

Even though she was used to going it alone, Sasha wasn't going to lie – his warmth was comforting.

Sasha stepped through the door, and even she could feel the thin membrane of magick that wrapped The Nest. As soon as she stepped through, everything disappeared except for her parents.

It was as though someone had thrown a switch and turned the lights off, except for one flickering beam shining down on where her parents sat, their eyes darting every which way as they tried to figure out what was going on. Everything else fell away to darkness.

Sasha crossed the room and stood in front of them, wondering if they could see her, trying to figure out what clues she was supposed to take away from this oddly orchestrated moment.

"Sasha?" her mother asked, pushing her hair away from her face and looking at her in confusion. Neither of her parents rose to hug her.

"What are you guys doing here?" Sasha said, carefully watching them, looking for signs of a silver glow or any sort of trickery. Though she hadn't had the best upbringing with them, she wouldn't be able to live with herself if she killed one of them thinking they were Domnua masquerading as her parents.

"Having a cup of tea. What are you doing here?" her mother said, looking around in bewilderment. Sasha glanced over her shoulder but all she saw was darkness.

"I was in the area. I thought I'd stop in. This was my favorite place growing up – did you know that?" Sasha asked, watching them carefully for any clue.

"Was it?" Her dad furrowed his brow as he thought about it. "I knew you were always riding off somewhere or the other, but wasn't sure where."

"I think I knew that you came here. You mentioned it a few times," her mom said.

"You didn't really know much about me at all, did you?" Sasha asked, narrowing her eyes at them.

"You never let us in. We didn't really know what to do with you. You were just so different than us," her mom said, shrugging helplessly.

Sasha's mouth dropped open a bit. All the old angst wanted to pour through and she forced herself to breathe for a moment, her eyes still darting around the table. Why couldn't she hear her friends behind her? What kind of bubble of magick was being cast around them?

"That's fair," Sasha decided to say and saw the look of surprise in her mother's eyes. "But does being different mean I should be shut out? You knew I was different. I was a foster. Why did you agree to take me in if you didn't want another child?"

"We didn't want you," her dad blurted out.

Sasha felt the rejection slice through her before it settled around the truth that she had already known.

"But we loved you nonetheless," her mom said, putting a hand out to her dad.

*To him, not to me*, Sasha thought.

"Perhaps we look at love a little differently," Sasha murmured, glancing over her shoulder for her friends again.

"We gave what we could – what we were capable of," her mother protested.

Sasha let that settle for a bit, testing the weight of it and deciding what she would do with it. As a child, she would have railed against them in anger. As an adult, however, it was time for her to forgive.

"I understand that now. I understand that you didn't know how to parent a child like me – that you wanted me to be something that I wasn't. But it wasn't out of malice, and I forgive you for trying to mold me into something that I'm not. But all I've ever needed was the freedom to just be who I was without judgment. But I'm happy now. I'm happy with who I am, the woman I've become, and the life I've created for myself. I'm proud of it," Sasha said softly.

Her mother looked at her in confusion. "Of course, we're very proud of you. That's all we've wanted, is your happiness."

Maybe it was just something Sasha was going to have to come to terms with – the fact that her parents might never understand her, but at the very least they did want what was best for her, even if their parenting style had been questionable at best. Because sometimes, that's all people can do – the best they know how, with the hand they were dealt.

"Tell me about where I came from," Sasha asked,

pinning her eyes on her father, who looked toward the wall, fidgeting with his collar.

"An old woman approached us. You were but a babe," her mother spoke, her brown eyes focused on the wall as she remembered. "We didn't want another child, you see? We couldn't afford one and didn't want the burden. But the promise was that if we took you in, we'd never suffer for anything again. And we haven't, not really. Though money was tight, our needs were always met. I think we argued too much back then because we didn't trust that things were going to work out. We also didn't really understand this child that had been given to us or the touch of otherness she carried with her." Her mother shook herself as though coming out of a trance and then flushed slightly, refusing to meet Sasha's eyes. "Frankly, you terrified us."

"Why did I scare you?" Sasha insisted.

"You weren't of this world. Your eyes would shift colors sometimes. Strange things happened around you. Yet, you never got hurt. You'd fall and not break anything. You'd dance out into the street in front of a car and the car would never hit you. You ran full speed ahead all the time and nothing ever seemed to get in your way. Yes, you're terrifying. So we did the best we could with someone we didn't understand and the powers we couldn't comprehend," her father said, his blue eyes meeting hers, making eye contact for the first time in this conversation.

"Why didn't you say anything to me?" Sasha asked in astonishment. But at the same time, she remembered the incident with the car that he referenced. She'd felt herself whisked out of the car's path. But by whom? Glancing over her shoulder again into the darkness, she wondered if it had been Declan, if even back then he'd protected her.

"It wasn't our place. There was no way to explain what we understood, but had no facts to back up," her mother shrugged.

"We did the best we could," her dad repeated.

Sasha looked at them with a new light, the old anger seeping away from her as though someone had opened a valve and let it pour out of her very soul. Holding onto that resentment did little for anyone. Her parents had done their best, and she'd still found her own way. Maybe, just maybe, they could have a new relationship now. One forged in understanding and respect, and not couched in past hurts and old patterns.

"You did just fine. I understand more, now that you've explained. Thank you for telling me," Sasha said gently.

"You always were in the light. Stay on the side of the light," her mother murmured, her face creased in confusion as if she were trying to remember something from long ago. "Ah, yes. That was it. The old woman said to go to the place of the light. No, where the light overcomes the darkness?" She drummed her hands on the table as Sasha's dad ran a hand through his hair.

"Where the light always shines," her dad clarified and they both beamed at each other, happy for remembering.

"Go to the place where the light always shines," Sasha repeated, then gasped when her parents disappeared before her, leaving not a trace behind, and the darkness fell away to reveal a full-scale battle around her.

"Sasha!" Bianca shrieked.

Sasha gasped as she was hit from behind.

# CHAPTER 26

"Where the hell have you been?" Declan growled into her ear as they rolled beneath a table, his body instinctively cushioning hers from the hard floor. A battle raged above them, with Domnua and Danula clashing swords desperately. Sasha gasped as Bianca flew by and launched herself at the back of a Domnua that had a chokehold on Seamus.

"What – what is going on? What happened?" Sasha asked, pulling away from Declan with the dagger in her hand as she tried to track the flurry of movement that coursed around them.

"It was like you just disappeared. You stepped inside and blinked out of sight. We had nothing to go on – nobody could find you. And then the Domnua slipped through the windows and before you know it, we didn't have time to look for you. We were too busy trying to fight for our lives. Luckily, just before you reappeared, we were given backup. It was quite literally like a switch was thrown and the Danula dropped from the air to help. I wonder what happened," Declan said, his breath tickling her ear as he panted, his arm still slung around her as they watched the battle.

Sasha knew what had happened. It was when she'd let go of the old anger and resentment and had decided to just view her parents as people who had done the best they could. She'd viewed it as a valve turning and releasing, but she supposed it could have been flipping a switch.

"You two having a cuddle mid-battle? I'll remember this next time you make me get out of bed with Bianca early," Seamus poked his head, upside down, at them beneath the table and shot them a cheeky grin before turning away to stab a Domnua.

"I suppose we should help," Sasha said, pulling away from Declan's warmth.

"Wait, where were you? Are you all right, then?" Declan tugged her braid back, making her pause for a moment as she looked into his eyes.

"Aye, I'm just fine. I had to let go of some old stuff. And I've got a new clue. Let's take care of this mess and I'll fill you all in," Sasha said, feeling lighter than she had in years. She crawled from beneath the table and leaped into the fray, her dagger sending little jolts of fire through any Domnua that dared to come too close. In a few short moments, they'd finished off the Domnua.

The remaining Danula bowed as one, a purply glow of otherness surrounding them, before they slipped from sight.

"It's weird that they bowed to us," Sasha said.

"You're saving their very world – they had best bow. You're like a princess," Bianca panted, then launched herself at a surprised Sasha, wrapping her arms tightly around her waist.

"Hey, it's fine. I'm alive, see?" Sasha held up her arms, but Bianca held on for a moment longer.

"You gave us a good fright, that's for sure," Maddox said, his face filled with annoyance as he wiped silvery blood from his blade.

"It wasn't my choice. I just stepped in and everything faded to darkness except for my parents sitting at the table." Sasha looked around her beloved shop, wondering if they would be able to put to rights all the damage inflicted in the battle. Tables lay splintered, glasses broken, and even one of the pretty stained-glass windows was shattered.

"We'll fix it. Promise," Seamus said, catching her look and patting her shoulder.

"What happened with your parents?" Maddox asked, concern in his eyes. He knew that she had often struggled with them.

"I think I needed to see them in a new light, and to release some old resentments that had hung on for too long. In the end, they gave me a clue." Sasha shrugged. "Though it makes little sense to me."

"What is it?" Declan asked.

She turned to look at him, then quickly looked away. *My, but the man was sexy.* Even more so after battle with adrenaline surging through her system. He looked all sorts of powerful, his hair mussed, his eyes predatory as they scanned the room.

"Sasha?" Bianca asked, and Sasha cursed herself as she pulled her eyes away from Declan.

"Go where the light always shines. The place. The place where the light always shines," Sasha amended, annoyed with herself for feeling flustered.

"What could that mean?"

"Heaven?" Bianca wondered.

They all looked at her, and Bianca shrugged. "What? It was the first thing that popped into my head. I thought we were brainstorming here."

"I think it needs to be a place we can go without, you know, dying to get there," Maddox said.

Bianca smiled at him. "Fine, but I'm saying that answer would work in pub trivia."

"Aside from answers to trivia night at the pub, anyone else have ideas?" Sasha asked, hands on hips as she continued to survey the damage to The Nest. It hurt her heart to see the place in shambles, but she trusted Seamus when he said they would fix it. Somehow.

"Hmmm, light always shines… a reflection? A mirror? Fire? The water? I know!" Bianca said, dancing around and waving her hands like she'd just won the lottery. "A lighthouse!"

They all paused at that.

Declan slanted Sasha a look.

"What does your gut say?"

She appreciated that he paused to check in with her and see how she felt, though it felt like incredible pressure on her shoulders to lead a mission she'd only recently learned she was a part of.

"It feels right," Sasha finally said.

"Yes!" Bianca clapped.

"Now which lighthouse?"

"Oh," Bianca said, looking so crestfallen that Sasha had to laugh.

"We'll figure it out. For now, let's move. It's not safe to stay here," Declan said, and they all filed out to the car. Sasha looked wistfully over her shoulder at the mess, but Maddox put his arm around her and steered her away.

"It'll be made right. I promise."

That was all she could hope for. It was the only place she'd ever really felt at home.

# CHAPTER 27

Sasha opted to stay in the car, and Declan remained with her while the other three ran into the market for provisions. They had yet to decide upon a direction for the night, but one thing they all agreed on was that they were ravenous.

Battle will do that to a body.

Sasha looked over at Declan. He was sprawled loosely on the seat, his broad shoulders and long legs taking up too much space, making her feel tiny in comparison. She'd slid across to the other side of the back seat so that she wasn't tucked against him while they waited for everyone. Her mind seemed to wander when she was in close quarters with him and she needed to be focused.

The sooner they found this sword, the sooner she could move on with her life.

"What happened with your parents?" Declan asked and Sasha glowered at him. That was right, she had a question that was bothering her.

"How long did you say you've been protecting me for?" Sasha queried back, ignoring his question.

"A handful of years. Why?" Declan shrugged, not really answering the question.

"A handful is – what, three years? Five years? Fifteen years?" Sasha asked, crossing her arms and refusing to look away.

"A while. What does it matter?" Declan said, irritation flashing over his handsome face briefly. He'd smoothed his hair back into its band at the nape of his neck and his cheekbones stood out in the light that slanted through the windows. He was probably one of the most perfectly built men Sasha had ever seen. The more she was around him, the more she found herself catching her breath – just a quick inhale – when she remembered just how beautiful he was.

"I asked you a simple question. I don't see why you can't just answer it," Sasha said, studying her nails for a moment before glancing back at him and waiting in silence.

"Since childhood," Declan finally said, and Sasha straightened in shock.

"Excuse me? How could you have protected me when you were a child?"

"That is when training begins. Others go with to mentor you. It's a rite of passage. But I've been alone since I was about this high or so." Declan held out a large palm to indicate height and shrugged again, clearly uncomfortable with the topic.

"You've known me my whole life? You've watched me? Oh! Even when I was so awkward? All by myself?

Playing behind the walls? Fencing invisible enemies?" Sasha slapped a hand to her face and groaned. Talk about embarrassment. He'd probably seen her cry more than a dozen times, or concoct imaginary friends to play with, or practice kissing on a pillow. Was there no end to her shame?

"You were the prettiest thing I'd ever seen. Still are," Declan said softly.

Sasha peeked at him between her fingers. His eyes were on hers, the corners softened as he looked at her with what she could only assume was kindness.

Or pity for the lonely young girl.

"I feel at a distinct disadvantage knowing you've been watching me my whole life, yet I know nothing of yours," Sasha said, her voice soft as she lowered her hands and looked at him.

"What do you want to know?"

"Where are you from? What is your family like? What would you be doing for a job if you didn't do this? What is your favorite music? Do you like chocolate?" The questions tumbled out before Sasha even realized they were out of her mouth, and she snapped her lips shut as Declan started laughing.

"Fae love sweets. So, yes, I love chocolate. I'm from a part of Ireland not known to humans, but let's say close to the Ring of Kerry. My family is loving, boisterous, and in each other's business constantly. My parents are immensely proud that I've been chosen for this task and they brag to all who will still listen to them. If I didn't do this, I would most likely do something on the water as I have a strong liking for the ocean. As for my favorite music, well, I'm partial to classic rock. There—did I answer all your questions?" Declan said, his grin flashing white in his face.

Sasha found herself feeling that funny little catch of breath again.

"So you'd be a sailor listening to Led Zeppelin and wooing all the ladies with your sweets?" Sasha asked lightly, but the image of him with a big happy family and loving the water tugged at her heart.

This man had been following her for her entire life and knew her in a way that she wasn't comfortable with. It was best for her to remind herself that he was fae – not human – and not try to fantasize about a relationship with him. Damn her hormones for making her want just a taste more of his touch. It was obvious she'd gone too long without dating someone, and certain of her more primal urges were in need of tending.

"Perhaps. But that is not my destiny. You are," Declan said, his eyes on hers again.

"See, this is what I don't get," Sasha said, annoyed with him again. "You keep claiming that I'm your destiny, yet you aren't interested in kissing me or dating me or anything like that. How can you possibly say I'm your destiny when you won't even touch me?"

A smile flashed across Declan's face, though a hungry look snuck into his eyes as he slowly ran his gaze up and down her body.

"So you want me to touch you then?"

"I didn't say that!" Sasha squealed, and then tamped down on the screech in her voice. "I'm just saying that you've not made a move or anything. So I find it highly unlikely that I'm your destiny. It's a little ridiculous. Especially considering that although you think you may know me, I don't know you at all."

"Good things come to those who wait," Declan said.

Sasha actually clenched her fist as she thought about punching him. Just lightly. Maybe right in that smug face of his.

"Who says I'll wait?"

Declan laughed at her and patted her knee gently. "You've got quite the sulk going on over there. Am I not paying enough attention to you? Maybe I need to spend more time letting you get to know me so you can get comfortable with the idea of us. Because once this mission is over, there will be an us."

"There will be no us. I've decided not to pursue this. I'm certain you've heard the term 'hell hath no fury like a woman scorned'? Well, I don't need to be turned down anymore. I'm no longer interested in you," Sasha said, turning to stick her nose in the air and ignore him completely. What was taking them so long anyway? It's not like they needed food for a party of twenty people.

She gasped as she was lifted, and in seconds found herself sprawled inelegantly across Declan's lap, her legs straddling him, his hands at her waist as he took her lips in a punishing kiss. This kiss – oh, this kiss was all of him. Where before had been but a taste, now he poured all his heat into it and Sasha went dizzy against his chest as he held her, prisoner to his will, and erased every conscious thought from her head but one.

This man.

They broke apart, both panting, each slightly angry and

more than aroused. Sasha slid awkwardly off of him and rushed back to the corner of the seat, crossing her arms over her chest to stare out the window again, refusing to touch her lips though they pulsed with wanting more of his kisses.

"That did not seem disinterested," Declan said mildly.

"Oh hush."

# CHAPTER 28

"What'd we miss? Were you guys making out? Did you have a fight? I sense something here," Bianca said immediately upon opening the door, circling one finger in the air at the both of them.

"I'm hungry," Sasha said, pointing at the bag Bianca held, "And I get cranky when I'm hungry."

"Hmmm. I'm doubting that is the case, but I'll leave it be for now," Bianca said and tossed a package of biscuits at Sasha, who immediately tore them open and crunched down without even looking at the flavor. Anything to distract from where her mouth just had been – and still wanted to be.

Maddox opened the door and eyed her, and she reluctantly slid across the seat until she was just a hint away from being pressed against Declan. Ignoring him, she offered Maddox a biscuit. It took all her willpower not to kick Declan when he looped his arm loosely over the back of seat so that his fingers hung lightly on her shoulder.

"Sorry to be a downer, Sasha, but I feel like we kind of

need to unpack the parent stuff," Bianca said, turning to give her a sympathetic smile. "I know it might be a weird thing to delve into, but there was a purpose for that whole set up."

"I've been thinking about that, actually. I feel like when there was a turning point in our conversation was the same instant that the Danula were able to come through and help you."

"Now, isn't that interesting," Maddox murmured next to her. "You passed some kind of test? You unlocked something?"

"Basically I looked at them as humans, doing the best they could in a tricky situation, and let go of any under-lying anger I had for them. Or perhaps I just changed my expectations of them. Either way, there was a level of forgiveness that I was working through, I suppose. But I felt it. Viscerally. And it was almost like a flood of nega-tivity leaving me."

"And I bet that was the exact time the Danula could get through to help us," Bianca said.

"Maybe she's a conduit? The more closed off or resentful she is, the less able she is to accept help. Or, you know, her destiny," Declan said, and Sasha entertained a brief fantasy of trying out her newfound firebolt power on him. Maybe not to really hurt him – just a singe. It was clear she needed to get a handle on her anger, as that was twice now that she'd thought of maiming him, just today.

"Resentful? Excuse me, I resent that," Sasha huffed and then just closed her eyes, shaking her head slightly as the car went dead silent. She counted to three. "Go ahead and laugh. I won't murder you. This time."

The car erupted in laughter, and Sasha found herself smiling too. Hey, if she couldn't laugh at herself once in a while, then what was the point of all this?

"I feel like this is a board game or, like, legend stuff," Bianca mused as Seamus pulled out and began to drive – to where, they did not yet know. "It's as though you pass a personal test, and then the next clue gets revealed. It's very old school mythological-type stuff here. I think it fits perfectly. Remove childhood angst? Forgive parents for perceived wrongs? Check. Here's your reward. Move to the next level."

"Sounds also like the way karma works – or past life stuff," Maddox mused.

Bianca nodded over her shoulder enthusiastically as she nibbled on a crisp. "Yes, like she was carrying guilt or anger from a past life that needed to be addressed, and once that gets released – on to the next level."

"Exactly."

"Are you saying that the more personal issues that I work out, the more clues will be revealed? It sounds like one big psychotherapy session, which is something I'm not exactly interested in going through," Sasha said. "In case you forgot, there are Domnua trying to murder us out there. We don't exactly have the time to peel away all my unresolved issues to get to the next level of the game, as you say. This is life or death."

"But maybe the issues you're dealing with are life or death too – to *you*," Bianca pointed out.

Sasha narrowed her eyes at her. "I find that highly unlikely," she said, finding herself wanting to bite her nails. It was an old habit, one that she had worked for years to overcome. The urges came about now when she was deeply vexed. She assumed it was like the craving for a cigarette after having a big fight with someone or when a person was stressed – something habitual to self-soothe. And just why, Sasha wondered, did she feel the need to self-soothe?

"Just exploring every angle, sweetie. Don't get too fussed about it," Maddox said, patting her leg gently.

Sasha turned to smile at him. She really needed to not be the cranky one holding everything up. As she was being constantly reminded, they were all in this together.

"I was thinking about the lighthouse as the place where the light always shines, but I don't think it is a modern-day working lighthouse. There's an old ruin, further down from Kinsale, along the coast into the Ring of Kerry. It used to be quite the fortress, but has been left in disrepair and fallen into ruin through the centuries. At the crest of the hill there's what would have been a lighthouse for its time, but it's no longer operating. I think part of it has fallen down as well. For some reason, that keeps sticking out to me when I think about 'lighthouse.'"

"Would you be able to direct us?" Seamus asked over his shoulder.

"Aye, I can direct you. I spent a lot of time there as a child. My family went on holiday near there and I would climb the hills until I could run free in the ruins."

"Another link then," Bianca murmured.

Sasha met her eyes. "Aye, another link."

"Time to storm the castle then."

# CHAPTER 29

*D*eclan kept his gaze out the window at the passing Irish countryside, caught in the middle between winter and spring, where yellowed grass turned to green and the beginning buds of new life poked from the ground. It was kind of like watching Sasha struggle to find herself again after the hits she'd taken in life. Each hit left her wobbly as a new foal learning to walk but, in a matter of time, stronger than ever as it loped across the fields.

He wanted to cheer her on – each and every time she'd picked herself up and kept going. Declan had a fiercely protective and proud attitude toward her, and not just because he was her protector. It was from watching who she had become, from a lonely and tentative slip of a girl to a fiercely resilient woman who could still offer kindness and forgiveness when needed. Had she grown cold over the years, he would have struggled with his feelings for her.

But to continue to see that huge heart under her iron-coated exterior? It was enough to make him want to break down the walls and hold her until she knew once and for all that she was loved unconditionally. Indefinitely.

Forever.

Declan felt his heart clench every time he thought about making this woman his. Not just in body, but in spirit and heart. She was the missing half that would make him whole, and a life without her by his side would be a life not worthy of living.

He had but to bide his time, find the sword, fulfill his oath. Only then would she be his.

If he could last that long.

Declan almost cursed out loud as he thought about hauling her into his lap and claiming her with his kiss. She'd responded instantly, not holding anything back, and he'd almost lost his mind. His fierce warrior, who protected herself so, did not lie about her passion or her feelings. She could've pretended disinterest or pushed him away. Instead she'd poured herself into the kiss and given of herself freely.

She was like a wildflower that drooped in the rain but held its face to the sun.

One day he would be her light, he promised himself. One day.

# CHAPTER 30

"This is it?" Seamus asked, indicating a small lane that turned off of the main road. They'd driven for several hours, Declan scanning the horizon for Domnua, while Bianca had bounced around theories on the sword. They'd come to no further conclusions, but several theories prevailed. Bianca was sticking with her belief that more clues would be revealed as Sasha worked through her personal issues. The thought of unpacking all her deep-rooted insecurities or personal issues made Sasha want to run for the hills and never look back.

"Aye, though the lane will only go so far," she said. "Then we'll need to walk. And since it is nearing dark, we'll want to bring our gear. In all likelihood, we'll be camping here tonight."

"We'll need to set wards then," Seamus said, sending a look at Declan, who only nodded his assent.

"Oh, can I watch? I've been dying to see how it's done," Bianca squealed.

"Anything for you, my beauty," Seamus said and Bianca sent him a glowing grin.

"I don't know if I like this. We're going to be virtually out in the open, and aside from our wards, unprotected," Maddox protested.

"Just wait until you see the keep. It is a ruin, but there is enough to provide some protection. It's not like we'll have to put tents out on the top of a hill," Sasha reassured him.

"Aye, but still. This is making me a bit tetchy," Maddox said.

"We'll figure it out. This feels right." It was all Sasha could say. It appeared that listening to her gut was what was supposed to guide this mission, so she was doing the best she could to check in with herself and make sure she was on point.

"Oh. Oh, just... oh wow," Bianca breathed as they crested a hill and the old ruin of the castle came into view. As ruins went, it was larger than was typical for Ireland, having been somewhat preserved through the years before the nearby town had stopped trying to raise funds to save it.

Three walls of what must have once been a fierce castle still stood proudly against the sky, where the sun had begun its journey to the horizon. Protected from the wind on most sides, the wall that had crumbled looked out over steep cliffs that jutted proudly into the water. A lone tower, presumably once the lighthouse, leaned slightly, but still held its perch at the very tip of the cliff. In the dimming light it looked fierce and, at the same time, so very lonely.

One sentry, left to shine its light, to protect them all.

"It's really lovely," Sasha agreed, her childhood memories of scampering over the walls and running the hills freely coming back to her. She looked at Declan. "You'd remember this place. Seeing as how you followed me even then."

"I remember," Declan said, his eyes still out the window.

"What does that mean?" Bianca asked.

"Declan has been protecting me for longer than I thought. Since childhood. So he got to see me at all my awkward stages," Sasha said stiffly.

"Oh my god, I love that! Isn't that just so sweet?" Bianca gushed, her hand at her heart.

"I would've protected you back then if I had known you," Seamus said, "I bet you were just the most darling child."

"Nope, chubby and awkward too. I think we all are as kids, though. Isn't that the thing? Everybody takes time to blossom," Bianca said.

"I don't know about you, honey, but I've always been fabulous," Maddox sniffed and Sasha laughed, not doubting that for a minute.

"I was awkward too. All legs and elbows and string-bean thin. Now I'm much more masculine," Seamus said, lifting a still-thin arm to flex it and causing the car to break into laughter.

"We'll set up camp in the corner here," Declan indicated, bringing them back to the present. Seamus drove the SUV as far as he could before the uneven terrain prevented them from going further.

"This is going to be so cool," Bianca exclaimed.

They gathered the gear from the car, Declan standing watch, then began to hike the hill that led to the ruin. The last light of the sun coated the hills in its wintry warmth and reminded Sasha they would need light.

"We need fire," Sasha said and Bianca nodded her agreement.

"We picked up wood at the market. I suspected we might be out in the cold. It was part of what was taking us so long."

"I was wondering what you were doing in there for all that time."

"Honestly, I could've bought more stuff but forced myself to stop. I didn't quite know where we would end up, but if it was outside? Especially this time of year, I knew we'd want the warmth. Plus Seamus said he knows some fae magick that will help keep a fire lasting longer, so we're lucky on that front." Bianca's breath puffed a bit as they hiked the incline, packs on their backs and arms full of supplies.

If the Domnua attacked now, they'd make quick work of the both of them, Sasha thought, and she moved the supplies to one arm so her hand could be free to grab her dagger.

"It's nice to have a magick element added to this quest, though it also works against us because the Domnua have magick. But I can't say I'm complaining about having some magick to assist us in a pinch, either," Sasha agreed as they neared the first wall of the castle.

"Yeah, yeah. Okay, dish. What's going on with you and Declan? You looked like you were going to eat each other alive when I got back to the car." Bianca zeroed in on the important stuff.

Sasha debated brushing it away, but her gut told her that she could use a friend. And so, trusting her instincts, she decided to open up.

"We argued. I discovered that he had been following me since childhood, which makes me feel super insecure and awkward, just thinking about all the dumb moments he probably saw of me. So we argued, and I told him that I wasn't going to be interested in him, and then he just hauled me into his lap and kissed me until I couldn't think straight," Sasha said in a rush. There, she was confiding.

"Oh. Well, can I just say 'yum'?" Bianca said, a dreamy look in her blue eyes as she imagined the moment. "Not that I'm not over the moon about my Seamus, but Declan is drop-dead delicious. I think you and every woman with breath still in her body would be lying if they said they weren't interested."

"Sure, he's nice to look at. But that's where it needs to stop," Sasha insisted as they approached the part of the wall that had crumbled to the ground. The wind picked up here and Sasha was grateful that Bianca had thought to bring firewood.

"Why?" Bianca asked.

"Because apparently he thinks I'm his destiny, but he refuses to act on it until the sword is found. It's like so long as I fall in line and do my part, then I get him as a reward." The thought had rankled Sasha for a few hours now, and saying it out loud annoyed her even more.

"I'm not sure I'd look at it that way. He seems incredibly dedicated to this job and this mission. Perhaps it's just that he wants to make sure he doesn't let you or anyone down – you know, by getting distracted on the job?"

"I doubt that. I think he wants to win," Sasha said, her tone grumpy.

"Well, duh, we all want to win. If we lose, we die." Bianca shook her head, her blonde hair bouncing off her shoulders.

"I just… I really am struggling with this concept that my destiny is all just laid out for me. Pre-ordained. What about free will? What about choice?" Sasha demanded, stopping to look at Bianca.

"You have it. You can go. Right now. Walk away. You may die, but there is nothing any one of us can do to stop you from going. Nobody is forcing you on this path. Everything is a choice. It's just that choices have consequences, no matter which side you fall down on."

"And no matter what, you live with those consequences," Sasha muttered, thinking of the choices that had been made for her in her life and the choices she had made on her own. Both had delivered different results, and both she'd had to deal with one way or the other.

"Yes, you do. You live with them, you push them away, you numb them, you work through them, or you accept them. But there is always a choice."

"I think this is important," Sasha said.

"Of course it is." Bianca shrugged.

"No, conceptually. To this mission. Just remind me to think on it later by the fire. For now, we need to set up camp before dark."

Choices, Sasha thought, as they entered the centuries-old ruin. It comes down to choices.

# CHAPTER 31

"You know, there are a lot of rooms and chambers and twists and turns to this old place," Maddox said, appearing around the corner of the wall with his arms full of wood. "A body could explore for days."

"I know. I have. Probably past the point where it was safe for me to do so," Sasha said, as she set up a tent in the corner of the ruin. She'd done her best to clear out the rocks and gravel, but it was still going to be uneven ground for sleeping on.

"Do you think the sword is here?" Maddox asked, and Sasha looked at him in surprise as she unrolled the canvas.

"Me? How would I know?"

"Aren't we following your gut instincts here? Wouldn't you be the first person to ask?" Maddox queried back.

Sasha paused as a bright flash of purple light, followed directly by Bianca's delighted laugh, shimmered over the open wall above them.

"The wards?"

"Aye, they are setting up a protective barrier. Though I don't think I'll be sleeping easy tonight. Not after the last two attacks," Maddox admitted. He bent and began efficiently stacking the firewood by a small hole Sasha had dug with a garden trowel she'd found in one of the packs. It wasn't pretty, but would do well enough to hold the fire. They needed light and warmth, that was for sure, as the wind had kicked up.

"I don't think any of us will sleep much until this is over. And to answer your question, yes, I think this feels right. For whatever that's worth." Sasha shrugged as she flattened a tarp over the ground to protect from dampness seeping in. "I suppose it would make kind of poetic sense though, right? Like finding the sword in an old castle. It's all very romantic and mythological. It would make sense to me."

"We fae do love our drama," Maddox admitted, coming over to help with the corner of the tent. They made short work of setting up the three tents and once again Sasha wondered where Declan would sleep. Or if he even needed sleep at all.

"Should we bunk together? So Declan doesn't feel the need to hide again like he did last night?"

"I wasn't hiding," Declan said from behind her, making her jump. She thought she'd be aware of his presence by now, since her skin seemed to tingle when he was around, but he still continued to sneak up on her.

"Seemed like it," Sasha said, unable to resist needling him.

"I was standing guard," Declan said stiffly.

"So you saw Clodagh pack up and leave and said nothing?" Sasha demanded.

"There was nothing to say. It isn't my job to question the motives of those who have served their purpose and wish to leave quietly. I told you she was protecting her clan. I would have done the same. Why are you so focused on this?"

"Because she abandoned me. Again!"

"You need to get over this abandonment stuff," Declan declared and Sasha's mouth dropped open. Maddox let out a long low whistle and made himself scarce.

"You don't get to tell me what to do. I'm finished with this conversation. Leave me alone," Sasha declared, her hands gripping the tent poles so tightly she was amazed they didn't snap in half.

"I won't leave you alone," Declan said, "and you will finish this conversation."

"I most certainly will not. What *you'll* finish is putting up these tents," Sasha tossed the poles at him and he caught them reflexively, his eyes flashing danger at her. "I have to use the toilet. I'd like privacy."

With that she stormed away from him and around the corner of the wall that offered shelter from the most bracing of the wind's chill. She walked headfirst into the wind, allowing the cold to numb her cheeks and to calm her temper as she stalked up the hill to another part of the castle, where she knew she could relieve herself in private. Not that she really had to go, but she damn well would, now that she'd made such a fuss of it.

Who did Declan think he was? He was trying to constantly force these conversations on her or make her think about things that she didn't want to discuss. If he was her destiny, well, she certainly wasn't interested in having herself dissected like that for the rest of her life.

No, she thought as she slipped through a small alcove into a sheltered hall with a grassy knoll on the other side. Not interested in the least.

# CHAPTER 32

*D*eclan paced, having set up the tents at lightning speed as he waited for Sasha to return. A part of him had wanted to follow her, but he knew when to give a woman space. Sasha had been bristling with anger and her need to be alone, so he had let her go. He hoped he wouldn't regret that decision.

"Bianca, can you just go check on Sasha? She went up the hill to the alcove to use the bathroom," Declan finally asked.

Bianca nodded, disappearing around the wall without a second question. Seamus watched her go and then met Declan's eyes.

"She'll be safe, right?"

"I believe so. The wards and protections we put up should hold," Declan said, and Seamus nodded. Maddox slowly stacked the firewood, using his knife to snap off bits and pieces to use as kindling until he had a little pile of wood shavings with a smaller teepee of sticks covering it. In moments, he had a cheerful little blaze going and had settled next to the fire, ready to tend to it and make sure it grew to a nice bed of coals so they could cook with it.

"Why are you forcing her to talk about things she doesn't want to talk about?" Maddox asked. Though the question was mild, Declan could read the underlying protective tone.

"Can't you see that's the quest?" Declan asked and both Seamus and Maddox paused to turn to him.

"How so exactly? I mean, I know we discussed her as a conduit perhaps for allowing the Danula to help or to go to the next level as Bianca mentioned, but what exactly are you saying?" Seamus asked.

"We're searching for the Sword of Light. Which is also known as the Sword of Truth. If the person who has to find it can't be truthful with themselves, then how are they ever to find it?" Declan asked, feeling like he was connecting the dots for children.

"Ohhhhhh, well. Now, isn't that interesting," Maddox murmured, and Declan almost threw up his hands but caught himself in time. No need to look like a dramatic woman, he thought, as he went about sorting their rations and getting the beginnings of a basic Irish stew together.

"You think if you push her to work through her personal stuff, the sword will be revealed? Or its location will be?" Seamus asked.

"I don't know if it will work like that exactly. But I don't think the sword will even remotely reveal itself to anyone who doesn't stand in their own personal truth. And until she lets go of some of her hang-ups, she'll never get there."

"Which makes you push her. I thought you were just

doing it because you loved her," Maddox said, standing and crossing his arms over his chest as he met Declan's eyes.

Declan read the challenge for what it was – a stand-in for a brother or a father, clearly asking what his intentions toward Sasha were.

"Aye, I love her. I have my whole life. It is only her for me. But I must wait until it is the right time to claim her. Or we will sacrifice the mission."

"Why? What could possibly make you think that?" Seamus asked, his face flashing confusion as he began to slice carrots onto a plate balanced precariously on his knee.

"I feel like I will be betraying my oath if I allow sex to distract me from the mission. I can't let down my guard," Declan said patiently, as though he was explaining to an addle-minded man.

"But you just said it was love. It's not just sex," Maddox said.

"It's not. But you're meaning sex and the consummation of a relationship. I won't go there until the sword is found."

"But what if it won't be found until you stand in *your* own truth?" Seamus asked. Declan stopped dead while Maddox let out a low whistle.

"I am standing in my truth," Declan said softly, his words a challenge.

"Are you? You've told her you love her?"

"She knows she's my destiny," Declan said, his hands clenching around the potato and knife he held.

"I don't hear the word love in there," Maddox said.

"Perhaps there is more to the puzzle than just what Sasha has to work through," Seamus said, his tone cheerful, "Hand over the potatoes if you're just going to hold them, or we'll never get food on tonight."

Declan absentmindedly handed him the potato as he thought about what they'd said. He was certain Sasha knew he loved her. That's what it meant when you told a woman she was your destiny. Right?

"Ah, feck," Declan swore and both men laughed.

"Ah, feck, indeed," Seamus said.

# CHAPTER 33

*A*n hour later, they crouched around the fire, some sitting on folded blankets, others on a log that Declan had dragged in from somewhere. The fire crackled merrily, its light dancing across the mossy stone walls behind them. Had the fate of the world not been on the line, Sasha might have been able to relax and enjoy the moment more.

Instead, she stayed tense, watching and waiting for the next thing to be sprung upon her. And the one making her the most nervous, aside from the possible appearance of the Domnua, was Declan himself. Ever since she'd stormed off and returned, he'd been overly attentive. Even now, he watched her across the fire, a new gleam in his eyes. It made her think that he wanted to peel back another layer, which was exactly what she didn't want to happen. Ignoring his look, she dug into the stew Bianca had just ladled out for her.

"For a basic camp stew, this is quite good," Sasha said to Seamus.

He nodded at Declan and said, "Declan's deserving your thanks, as he's the one who flavored it."

Of course the man cooks. Sasha almost rolled her eyes, but refrained.

"'Tis good," Sasha said, gesturing with her bowl at him. There. She'd been nice.

"Thanks, I made it with love," Declan said, his voice laced with heat, and Sasha did roll her eyes then.

"Dial it back, okay? I'm not mad from earlier. Just let it pass," Sasha said, deciding to address the elephant in the room.

"It is interesting that you're so prickly toward me if you've let things go, as you say," Declan said.

Sasha looked down at her stew. "I didn't realize this stew came with a side of attitude," she said, lifting the bowl and pretending to look deep inside it.

"The attitude's only coming from you, babe," Declan said and Sasha could feel her anger begin to boil. It was a good thing her dagger wasn't in her hand, as she might have been shooting fire bolts without meaning to.

"Don't 'babe' me, buddy," Sasha said, her eyes meeting Declan's over the fire. The flame reflected in his as he watched her carefully.

"Sooo, I'm just going to interject here," Bianca said cheerfully. "As much as I love to watch drama, I'm thinking we need to remember that we're all on the same team here."

"And I think if Sasha wants to be on the team, then she needs to start opening up. It's quite clear that we will keep throwing ourselves in the line of danger until she lets go of some old wounds. It is what the Sword of Light means – it is the Sword of Truth. The Seeker can't find it unless she is first truthful with herself," Declan said.

He spoke in an even tone, but his words felt like little bullets, each one hitting its mark, until Sasha wanted to just close her eyes and crawl into her tent and pretend that none of this was happening.

"Honestly, I think this is all a bunch of shite. It would make zero sense that generations of Seekers would all come down to the last Seeker before the curse ran out, having to be truthful about love or loss or whatever in order to find the sword. Think about it – there has to be something much more significant to finding this sword than my own personal issues. It's too... messy," Sasha said, finally deciding on the right word.

"Fae love tricky things though," Seamus said, holding his hand up to stop her from speaking again. "Also, you must understand the mercurial nature of cursed objects. They change, meld, absorb energy, or the curse takes new meanings through the centuries. It is part of what makes fae magick so fascinating, and also so difficult to deconstruct. And I think we were given a major clue with what happened with your parents. I'm sorry that this is uncomfortable for you, but we can't ignore it. It would be foolhardy to do so."

It irked Sasha that Seamus might be right. But what bothered her even more was what Declan had said – about repeatedly leading her friends into danger because she was unwilling to take a chance on opening up about her own buried issues.

"Show of hands how many people here think this is the key to finding the sword," Sasha finally said.

She was not surprised to see all hands raised around the fire.

"You swear you're not doing this just because you want to hear the dramatics of my life?"

"I mean, I do love a good drama. But not when I know it is going to hurt my friend to tell it," Bianca said gently. It was probably the most perfect thing she could have said to put Sasha at ease.

"Here, this may help," Maddox said, rummaging in a satchel at his feet and then pulling a bottle of Middleton from his bag.

"Aye, you're right at that." With no cups to be found, they ended up passing the bottle around, each taking a swig or two. Sasha let the heat of the whiskey warm her throat, trickling down until it settled into her core. She pulled the blanket tighter around her and stared into the flames, the wind sounding hauntingly like long-lost lovers calling for each other over the crashing waves.

The sky was clear, which made the light of the half-moon seem even brighter, yet oddly colder, as though the white light competed with the warm yellow glow of the fire. Sasha ignored the waves and the wind and the moon, and looked deep within the flames to where the hottest part of the fire danced in blue streaks. She'd always identified with fire. There was something about the all-consuming nature of it – the take-no-prisoners aspect – that the warrior in her respected. It wasn't entirely surprising to her that her gift of magick was fire.

"Well, we know abandonment is a big one. Which, for any kid raised as you were, is fairly normal," Bianca said, nudging the door open for Sasha.

"Do you just want me to talk about all the things I have issues with? Because that could take days. Like, for example, I hate that all the paper towel holders in bathrooms are too high for me and when I reach up to pull a towel the water runs down my wrists and under my sleeves. Every time."

They all looked at her like she was slightly crazy before breaking into laughter, which eased some of the tension that had tightened Sasha's shoulders. She rocked her head back and forth to loosen herself up a bit and then smiled as well.

"See what I mean?"

"I'd say maybe stick to the big ones. Like, it's obviously about love, abandonment, resentment, anger… you know, the things that trigger those kinds of feelings for you."

Sasha scrubbed a hand over her face and took a few calming breaths. These people were her friends, and if Declan was right about her continuing to lead them into danger because of her inability to open up about these things, well, she had a duty to perform then.

"Well, I think I worked through one of them already, when I was talking to my parents. I'd say some of that was anger and some of that was resentment. Which I suppose can be both sides of the same coin. And maybe I have a new perspective now on what they were dealing with and how I might have been a difficult child to connect with. So I don't know if we need to unpack that one too much more." Sasha shrugged and Bianca passed her the whiskey again.

"Abandonment sure seemed to set you off earlier

today. What about that one? You're scared to be alone?" Declan said, and Sasha glared at him through the flames.

"I am most certainly not scared to be alone. Hell, I've been alone for a while now. I've lived a lot of my life on my own – especially in a family that didn't understand or accept me for who I am. And that's the crux of abandonment issues. It's not that you're scared to be alone; it's that you wonder if you are going to be good enough for other people."

The wind kicked up even more and Sasha tugged the blanket around her, hating this moment.

"Of course you're good enough," Bianca said. "You're amazing. I'm proud to call you a friend."

Sasha smiled at her but shook her head.

"It isn't like that. It's more… will someone love the real me? See me for who I am? The good and the bad? And still stick around? And unfortunately, I've yet to really find that."

"Hey," Maddox said, his expression hurt across the fire. "I've stuck around."

"Yeah, and we're here," Seamus said.

"You guys haven't known me that long. But Maddox has, and I'm sorry, you're right. You have been there through all my bitchy moods. But see how tricky these issues are? Now, I wonder if you would have stayed if you hadn't been tasked with protecting me." Sasha shrugged helplessly under the blanket as hurt crossed her friend's face.

"Nobody made me protect you. Yes, it's been an honor being close to you and being able to help. But I wouldn't have done that if I didn't love you. Bitchy attitude and all," Maddox said evenly.

Sasha felt her heart constrict as his words registered. "I'm not trying to offend you, please know that," she said softly. "It's just the mind tricks that I play on myself."

"And then your fiancé cheated on you. So you view that as abandonment, when it actually has nothing to do with you and everything to do with him," Declan said evenly.

Sasha drew back in surprise. "Um, nice way to try and reframe it, but I'd say it has everything to do with me. Clearly, I wasn't meeting his needs."

"Or clearly the guy's simply a horse's arse," Seamus said, shaking his head. "Sorry, Sash, but I don't buy that for one bit. If someone cheats, that is their problem – their issue. Something is intrinsically wrong inside them and they go seek out something else to fill a void. But ultimately, they'll never be happy until they fill that void themselves or fix what is broken. It's a coward's way to leave a relationship. It causes too much hurt. Every man should have the integrity to stand up and say 'I'm unhappy and need to leave' instead of lying and sneaking around. That says a lot about the character of the man, though – not about you. You could be the best girlfriend in the world and if the man is broken, you can't fix that. You'll never fix that. He needs to fix himself. It has nothing to do with being good enough. In fact, you were probably too good for him and tried to help him for too long. But don't take that blame on you. That wasn't your choice and certainly wasn't your fault."

"See why I love this guy?" Bianca said, leaning over to

plant a big kiss on Seamus while Sasha just stared at him, dumbfounded, across the fire.

"And all this time I kept thinking it was me. Something I could've done differently," Sasha said.

"Aye, you could've done something differently," Declan said, and Sasha jerked her head up, eyes narrowed at him. "You could've picked a better man. That much you can own."

Sasha opened her mouth to spit anger at him – because what did he really know? Then she shut it and took a deep breath.

"You're right. I could've picked a better man. I guess I didn't see the signs when I should have. He was broken long before I got there and while I did what I could to help him learn and grow, ultimately, until he fixes himself he'll remain broken."

"And a horse's arse," Seamus reminded her.

Sasha physically felt a loosening inside of her, as though something was clicking open, and releasing. Similar to the flood of anger leaving her body earlier that day, a weight seemed to be lifted from her shoulders.

"Thanks, guys. I've never really looked at it like that. It's so much easier to be self-critical than it is to be critical of others."

"Oh really? Doesn't seem to stop you with me," Declan bit out and Sasha shot him a cheeky grin.

"You must bring out my bitchy side."

"I'll take any side you'll give me, my heart," Declan said, and Sasha felt heat lance through her, just before the sky exploded above them.

"Attack!" Bianca shrieked.

# CHAPTER 34

The Domnua dropped from the sky in hordes, riding winged beasts from mythological tales that caused Sasha's heart to skip a beat. Those sitting by the fire were separated instantly in a blur of silvery fae and Sasha screamed as she found herself launching into the air, thrown over the back of one of the beasts and being flown to the tower.

She twisted, trying to throw herself free before they enclosed her in the lighthouse, but the grip on her arm was so strong that she felt her shoulder begin to wrench out of the socket. Crying out in pain, she stopped struggling and dropped her head, assessing every detail and every movement as she waited for what would come next.

They'd entered the top room of the old lighthouse, where the wind whipped fiercely through the cracks in the stone and the walls were damp with ocean spray. Tossing Sasha on the floor, the Domnua stood above her and commenced to argue long and low, though Sasha caught a few words.

"Goddess Domnu says to take her alive," one of the Domnua argued, while the other two paced. Sasha barely moved, her eyes tracking them, as she inched her hand closer to where she hoped the dagger was still at her waist.

"But if we kill her, the curse is done. There is no other Seeker for the sword. We'll be heroes!" another hissed, this one long and lean and snakelike as he slipped across the floor, tossing evil looks her way.

Sasha almost let out an exclamation of happiness when her hand found the hilt of her dagger. It hadn't fallen in the flight to the tower. Her necklace remained on, humming warmth through her core, and she ordered herself to think, pausing to assess the situation as a warrior would.

The Domnua were clearly dismissing her as any threat; they often turned their backs on her as they paced and argued. She could take the one on the left out quickly, before he had a chance to turn, but the other two were wild cards. However, if she charged up her dagger with some of that newfound magickal fire power – maybe, just maybe, she could get to the other two quickly enough. Reminding herself of the fae's unnatural speed, she shifted just a bit so that she was able to bring herself to a squat, but kept herself in a ball as though she was still huddled and scared.

When the one closest to her turned his back to argue some more, she launched herself up, her dagger spearing through his back directly where his heart was. As silvery liquid rained everywhere, before the other two fae had time to react, Sasha called upon the heat in her core to lash out with a bolt of fire so bright it made her cry out in surprise as she obliterated the other two in one fell swoop.

But not before she felt a lance of pain in her side.

Looking down, she saw that one of them – the snake-like one – had managed to slice her with his dagger.

"Damn it," Sasha swore. Without thinking she pulled her shirt off and wrapped it tightly around her midsection, doing her best to stop the flow of blood. It looked like a fairly minor wound, but with fae magick in play, she had no idea what the outcome of such an injury might be.

Hearing shouts from outside, she raced to one of the open slots in the stone and pressed an eye to it to try and see. Unlike a traditional lighthouse, the windows were mere inches-wide openings in the stone, which Sasha imagined was to keep the flame of the fire going and protect it from the wind. But for now, it only provided annoyance as she tried to see what was happening far below her at the ruin.

The darkness was too impenetrable for her to see much other than flashes of purple and silver, but the purple glow made her feel better. The Danula had arrived and they were not alone down there. Now, all she had to do was find a way out of this lighthouse. Sasha paused for a moment and looked at her dagger, considering if she could use the magick through the window. But since she couldn't get a good read on what she was aiming at, she decided it was best not to. The last thing she needed to do was injure or kill one of her friends.

Her friends. The ones who were risking their lives for her. Because they thought she was worth it. That thought alone filled her with a love and a hope for the future that she hadn't felt in a very long time.

Sasha trailed her hand along the cool stone, circling in the darkness, trying to find a doorway out. There had to be a way out. Someone needed to climb the tower and light the flame, right?

She paused and looked toward the structure she could see just dimly in the middle of the room. Crossing to the structure she felt around almost blindly until she felt some sort of papery material, almost braided. Maybe a rope? Unsure of herself, but deciding to trust her instincts, she stepped back and aimed her dagger at it. She briefly wondered if her fire power would work when there was no immediate danger, but then pushed the thought away and summoned the same feeling in her core. In seconds, fire shot from her blade and ignited what indeed looked like a wick. The fire sputtered for a moment and then took life, filling the room with enough of a glow that Sasha could finally get her bearings.

"You know what? This is a very useful tool," Sasha said, looking down at her little dagger before studying the room around her.

She almost shouted in joy when she saw the door. Then she cursed again when she found it to be made of metal, and long since rusted over. The hinges, the lock, and the door itself were so covered with rust and salt that it had warped to the point of being unable to budge. No matter how many times Sasha threw her weight against it, she was stuck.

Briefly considering whether she could blast through it with her fire power, she decided against that. She had no idea what was on the other side and if one of her friends saw the light in the tower and tried to rescue her, she'd damn near take their head off.

Resigning herself to waiting, she went back to the

window, wrapped the blanket around her and pressed a hand to her wound while the battle raged below.

And prayed to the Goddess Danu that none would be hurt this evening.

# CHAPTER 35

*D*eclan whirled, mad with terror for Sasha, as he drove his sword through yet another Domnua. They'd been blessed with the warrior Danula arriving in time to stave off the majority of Domnua, but they were weakening and he'd yet to see where they'd taken Sasha.

His eyes scanned as he loped across the hill, slashing his way through Domnua after Domnua, not once looking back. He'd find her. It was his destiny to protect her, and the fact that she'd been taken before his very eyes was something he would never forget.

Nor forgive, he thought, as he neatly sliced the head off another Domnua.

Where was she?

A flicker of light, high on the horizon, caught his eye and he stilled. Was that flame in the lighthouse?

*Where the light always shines…*

Declan swore, but understood immediately what was being asked of him. He worked his way through the crowd of Domnua, stepping up his already inhuman speed to change the course of the battle. In a matter of moments, the tide had turned in their favor. Surveying the few Domnua left, Declan turned to yell to Maddox.

"She's in the tower. I'm going for her."

"Aye, we'll hold the ground. Go get our girl," Maddox shouted back, then leaped once more into the fray, his bracelets jingling madly from his arm as he fought. Declan found himself smiling – he had to admire a man who could dress for dinner and a battle in the same outfit.

Crossing the hill at a loping run, Declan reached the tower and circled it until he found the small door at the base. Putting his weight into it, he tried to push it open.

"No? Not going to let me in? Doubtful," Declan bit out. With one kick he slammed the door from its hinges, bursting the rusted metal into fragments. In seconds, he crouched through the opening and entered the dark stairwell, his sword drawn. When no Domnua immediately jumped him, he began his ascent, treading carefully on the worn stairs. With each step, the wood groaned beneath his weight and Declan slowed. Though he didn't want to sheath his weapon, he knew it would be foolhardy to not grasp the railing that was lodged into the stone. Narrowing his eyes so he could use his extra senses to see more clearly, he carefully ascended each step, praying he would find Sasha alive.

A musty damp scent clung to the walls and cobwebs brushed his face as he climbed, ever so slowly, the forced caution making him want to scream with rage. Sasha could be dead or dying, and it would be all his fault.

He would have failed his people.

And lost the love of his life.

# CHAPTER 36

"*S*asha!"

Sasha jumped as she heard a muffled shout from behind the door. She choked out a sob, beyond grateful that someone had come for her. They'd found her.

"I'm here! I'm safe!"

"Stand back from the door," Declan ordered and Sasha ran to the other side of the room, crouching behind where the flame still burned brightly in its stone holder in the middle of the room. She winced a bit at the pain in her side.

"I'm clear."

Even though she was prepared for it, the force with which the door shattered still caused her to jump.

"Where are you?" Declan raged, striding into the room, his eyes wild. She popped up from behind the wall, suddenly feeling shy when she saw the fierceness of his gaze.

"I'm here. Is everyone okay? Is anyone hurt?" Sasha

said, her hand automatically going to her side. She shivered when his gaze sliced over her, suddenly realizing that her shirt was off and tied around the wound in her side. Which meant she stood before him in her black lace bralette – one of her favorites, as it was pretty but serviceable, as she didn't need much support.

"You're hurt," Declan said, striding to her and immediately dropping to his knees in front of her to untie the shirt and examine the wound in her side.

"Um, well, yeah, I think just a slice. It stings, but nothing too bad, I'm sure."

"Fae wounds are tricky," Declan said, his hands tracing over her stomach and side, making her shiver.

"I know. But I think it will be fine. It just bled more than most to start. It's already closing." Sasha shrugged, keeping her eyes trained on the wall across the room. She was not going to look down. Not while he was kneeling at her feet with his hands at her waist. Nope. She bit her lip and kept her eyes straight ahead.

The silence dragged out between them. It seemed as though his hands warmed even more on her skin, digging gently into her waist, and she could feel his breath, coming out in soft little puffs just at her waist. Damn the man for being so tall, she thought, and kept her mind schooled on the battle that raged on the grounds below them.

And not the one that raged in her heart.

"Look at me."

It was a command, and one that she couldn't ignore. Sasha looked down to see Declan gazing at her, almost reverently, the fire in his eyes promising her everything she ached for.

"Declan, we can't…" Sasha was surprised to find her voice shaky, matching the tremor that now shook her legs.

"Choose me," Declan ordered, his voice hoarse, his eyes desperate with longing.

Sasha forced herself to look away, thinking of their conversation earlier and how he'd called her out for choosing the wrong man before. Could she trust herself to make this choice again?

"I thought I wasn't capable of making good choices," Sasha bit out, looking away from him. She gasped when he lifted her, slamming her against the wall so that her legs wrapped naturally around his waist. Her heart clenched and something tugged low and deep in her core as she pressed against his hardness.

"You chose wrong before. You learned your lesson. But you have to choose," Declan said, his voice husky at her throat.

Sasha bit back a moan as he trailed his lips down her ear, nibbling softly at the lobe before continuing his slow perusal of her neck, his lips trailing heat and slickness as he nipped and licked. She shivered against him, wanting to push him away and yet dying to pull him closer.

Sasha gasped as his mouth found her nipple through the thin layer of lace. Despite herself, she arched into his mouth, the cool stone of the wall pressing against her back, the heat of his mouth on her almost driving her crazy with need. Despite herself, she found her hips moving against him, her legs tightening to pull him closer.

"Choose." Declan's head reared up, his eyes fierce with anger and something more – both a challenge and a promise.

"Yes, Declan," Sasha gasped, and ran her hands through his hair to pull his mouth to hers. "I choose you."

"Mine," Declan declared against her mouth and then spoke no more as his tongue dipped in her mouth, dancing with hers, teasing and pulling back, mimicking the primal thrust of what her hips were currently doing against his hard length.

Declan broke away and dropped to his knees, and Sasha was again startled by their difference in height. Even on his knees, his mouth easily captured her nipple again. She moaned against him and threaded her hands through his hair, arching back as he made short work of removing her pants. Her legs trembled as his arms came around her, tenderly this time, tugging her gently forward until his mouth found the one place she ached for him most.

Lost, Sasha bowed back, riding the wave of pleasure as his tongue expertly took her up and over, her body breaking in waves of pleasure. He continued his even rhythm, his hands gripping her bottom as he continued his relentless pursuit of her body. It was only after she'd crested the sharp wave of pleasure once more that he pulled away and met her eyes.

"I need you," Declan said, his voice savage, and Sasha could only nod her assent before, once more, he picked her up, pinned her to the cool wall, and entered her in one smooth stroke.

It could have been minutes or hours. The flame in the middle of the room flickered softly, and Sasha, caught between the hard stone of the room and the hard wall of man holding her up, lost herself to him.

"My destiny," Declan breathed against her lips, over and over until she cried out, releasing herself, and her heart, for him to hold – no matter what battles lay ahead.

She'd been lost since the moment she'd seen him, anyway.

# CHAPTER 37

*S*asha allowed Declan to carry her down the staircase, though it made her feel slightly like the damsel in distress being rescued from the tower. But she couldn't deny that his vision was far better than hers and the stairs leading down were about to crumble beneath them.

She didn't exactly allow herself to snuggle into his arms, but she didn't hold herself stiff or away from him either. There was something distressingly vulnerable about being carried places, and yet part of her – dare she say, the damsel part – kind of liked it. She sighed and closed her eyes for a second, savoring the moment but also berating herself for enjoying this too much.

She was a trained martial artist, after all. It wasn't as though she wouldn't have figured out a way to get down the stairs. But her mind was still reeling from what they'd just done and how he had claimed her in a way that made her realize everything had changed. And that there was no going back.

"Sasha!" Bianca shouted as soon as they squeezed through the door. Sasha waited for Declan to put her down as Bianca and the others raced across the field, empty now except for the faint puddles of silvery blood, dimly reflecting the light of the moon.

"Put me down," Sasha hissed when Declan made no move to do so as she had expected.

"Are you wounded?" Bianca asked as she skidded to a halt in front of them, Maddox and Seamus close behind. "Oh, you're all flushed. If you're hurt, I hope a fever hasn't set in." Bianca began to cluck over her as Declan helped Sasha to her feet, where Bianca could bend over and assess the wound. Her cool fingertips pressed the skin of Sasha's abdomen as she looked for any other injuries.

"I'm going to do a perimeter check," Declan said, his tone gruff as he took off at his inhuman speed to check the wards and add other protection spells.

Maddox sized up Sasha briefly and then a huge grin split his face.

"Methinks her being flushed is not from a fever, my pet," Maddox told Bianca in a stage whisper, and Seamus chuckled. Bianca, blonde head bobbing up in confusion, looked between them all and then took a long look at Sasha's face.

"You did it with him!" Bianca squealed and Sasha slapped a hand to her face. Was there no privacy with this group?

"Could we not do this right now? I'm standing here in my bra and it's freezing out. Plus, I have been injured and I do think there is a wee bit of fae magick in this wound, so if one of you two could perhaps put something on it? It burns more than it did an hour ago," Sasha said.

Seamus and Maddox sprang into action. Maddox dragged his coat off and tossed it around Sasha's shoulders while Seamus ran for the keep.

"He's got a great bag full of magickal bits and whatnots," Bianca said, looping her arm through Sasha's as they hurried across the dark hill. "I've been dying to dig around in there and ask what everything is for, but he refuses to let me. I *will* get in there someday, though."

"I'm sure you only have to withhold sex and he'll hand it over in an instant. The man is besotted with you," Sasha said.

Bianca let out a peal of laughter that tinkled across the hilltops. "I would, but then I'd just be punishing myself as well. No sense in that, is there? He'll show me when he's ready to show me."

Sasha's teeth began to chatter as the wind grew colder, blowing up beneath the coat, and whatever fae magick had been on the dagger slowly seeped into her blood. Now she did feel as though a fever was overtaking her, and it wasn't a normal one.

"I don't feel so well," Sasha finally admitted, and Maddox scooped her into his arms without breaking stride, picking up the pace. They quickly arrived at the keep, where the fire still blazed and Seamus was stirring something in a pot hung over the flames.

"Quickly now," Seamus ordered, pointing to where he'd laid a sleeping bag by the fire. "Lay her there. I'll want to use a poultice as well as have her drink something."

Sasha began to shiver as she was put down on the sleeping bag, and she wondered if it was just coming down from the adrenaline of the past two hours, or if the fae magick was really affecting her so. Fierce battle was known to raise the adrenaline, which explained what had happened with Declan after. 'Twas natural to feel lusty when the adrenaline was still surging through her body. It couldn't be much more than that, Sasha tried to convince herself; she barely knew the man.

Liar, her brain whispered, and she shoved the thought down as shudders began to rack her body. It felt like ice was creeping through her veins. Dimly, she heard Bianca talking to her.

"Hey, I need you to stay with me here." Bianca was crouched by her head, holding a cup to her lips. Sasha gulped at the liquid, knowing that it would help her, but not even remotely wanting to swallow it. She reminded herself to be a warrior and take her medicine, so she did as Bianca instructed.

"Ouch," Sasha sputtered, as Seamus pressed a steaming poultice to her wound.

"I'm sorry, but it needs to be applied hot. Warmth to fight the cold, you see?"

Sasha nodded, and finished swallowing whatever bitter solution was in the cup that Bianca kept shoving at her face. When it was finally finished, she swatted the cup away and put her head down, only turning it to the side when she heard angry voices.

Her vision was beginning to blur. There must have been a sedative in the mixture, she thought, as she dully watched Maddox get in Declan's face.

"She's wounded. And you thought that was the right time to tup her?" Maddox shouted.

Declan's face went to stone when he saw Sasha lying on the ground. "Back off," he ordered, and Maddox shoved him, making Sasha's eyes pop open.

"You're supposed to protect her. Which means her welfare comes before your lusty needs," Maddox said, shoving him once more before turning to stalk over to Sasha.

The shattered look on Declan's face was the last thing Sasha saw before darkness claimed her.

# CHAPTER 38

*I*t was light the next time Sasha opened her eyes, and all she felt was an incredible sense of peacefulness. Cocooned in a sleeping bag, well-rested, she blinked as the tent around her rustled in the wind, which had yet to abate from the night before. Or was it several nights? She wondered how long she had been out.

"You're awake," Declan said, his lips pressed to her neck and Sasha jolted in her sleeping bag, instantly realizing the other reason she felt so safe. Declan's large arm was looped loosely around her waist and he'd pulled her back against him until his large shoulders overshadowed her slim ones.

"I... what are you doing in here? How long have I been out?" Sasha asked, feeling a blush creep up her cheeks as she remembered what they'd done right before the fae sickness had taken hold of her.

"Just through the night. I want to check your wound," Declan said.

Sasha found heat creeping up her cheeks once again as

he pulled the sleeping bag down and lifted her shirt to poke and prod at her abdomen. Luckily, she felt no pain when he did.

"It feels fine. Actually, I feel great," Sasha admitted, reminding herself to ask Seamus just what he'd given her. Now, she was just as curious as Bianca about what kind of tricks he had in his little magick bag.

Declan placed an arm on either side of her shoulders, effectively caging her as he loomed over her and looked deep into her eyes. Sasha's heart sped up as she lost herself for a moment.

"I'm sorry I failed you," Declan finally said, his tone serious, shame crossing his face.

"What? How did you fail me?" Sasha asked, immediately reaching up to press her hand to his face, her hand scraping against the coarse hair on his chin.

"I didn't protect you," Declan said, and she could feel his jaw clench as he spat the words out.

"But you did. You rescued me." Sasha was confused. He'd done everything he was supposed to do.

"And then immediately became consumed with my own needs and didn't tend to your injury," Declan said, derision in his tone.

"Hey, we thought I was fine. And you tended to my needs… quite well. Several times," Sasha said, already feeling the long languid pull of lust in her core as she thought about their time in the tower.

Declan's eyes turned predatory as he watched her, his breathing picking up – just a tick, but enough that Sasha sensed the switch from anger to lust.

This time it was Sasha who leaned forward, brushing

her lips across his in the softest of kisses. Both to reassure and to test herself, she explored gently, and Declan tilted his head, only opening his mouth slightly to allow her to dip her tongue in.

Gently, she lost herself, much like yesterday, as a feeling she wasn't sure she even totally understood came over her. In a matter of moments she'd threaded her hands through his hair and was gasping against his mouth, wanting so much more from him.

"Lass, I can't. You're injured. It would be dishonorable of me," Declan said, knowing what she wanted but still holding himself straight on his arms above her.

"I'm fine. I swear it. Whatever Seamus put in his magick concoction has healed me up," Sasha said, her eyes on him as insecurity crept in. Maybe it was best that they didn't do this again. The heat of the moment after battle was one thing, but having morning snuggles in a tent was oddly intimate. Perhaps her heart wasn't ready for this after all. "Never mind. I'm certainly not going to try and force myself on a man. It's fine."

Sasha moved to roll out from beneath him but found his arms would not budge. She glared up at his face.

"Let me go."

"Never," Declan whispered fiercely, claiming her lips with his, this time pouring all of the urgency he felt into it. In seconds, Sasha was riding the wave with him, unable to say no, unable to turn away.

And in the early morning hours, with the winds blowing and the misty Irish rain shrouding their tent, they loved each other as though they had known each other forever.

Destiny, Declan had kept repeating to Sasha. He touched her as though he knew her in a way that no others had or ever could again – and maybe, just maybe, he was right.

Would she be a fool to turn this gift away?

# CHAPTER 39

"*I* want to go back up into the lighthouse, now that the door is open. I feel like we could be missing something," Sasha shrugged, frustrated that they still had no direction and yet feeling incredibly languid after her morning with Declan.

"Do you not feel like the sword is here?" Bianca asked, blowing on the bowl of oatmeal before handing it over to Sasha, who took it eagerly. She felt like she could eat a meal for ten right now. Between the battle last night, whatever magick Seamus had given her, and her time with Declan, she felt like she had ten cups of coffee coursing through her veins.

"I don't know. I'm not sure what to look for. It seems foolish to stay here one more night, though, doesn't it? The Domnua know where we are, they know how to attack, and next time they may come in a different way. Shouldn't we keep moving?"

"I agree," Maddox said, coming from around the wall of the keep and hurrying over to cup Sasha's face in his hands. Measuring her with a long look, he saw what he needed and then bent to kiss her forehead. "Glad you're better now."

"Sorry to scare you for a moment there. I honestly was convinced that I was fine," Sasha said.

"Fae magick is sneaky like that. It has killed more than one in battle that way. They ride off, thinking they are fine, and the poison acts when they are too far away for help," Seamus said, poking his head from the tent before extricating his long limbs and standing to stretch, his red hair at all angles as usual.

"Thank you for your help. I feel right as rain this morning," Sasha said with a smile for him. "In fact, there's barely a mark on my stomach. I'm certain you could make billions if you patented that and sold it."

Seamus laughed and crossed to drop a kiss on Bianca's cheek before taking the oatmeal she offered.

"True, I most likely could. But my life is much easier this way. More money, more problems, as they say."

"Plus, you'd probably be violating all sorts of fae moral codes and whatnot," Bianca said, settling herself on the ground next to Sasha. The fire still sputtered cheerfully, and Sasha assumed it was also helped along with a little magick.

It was one of the misty gray mornings that Ireland was famous for, and the waves of mist being blown across them in the wind made Sasha think fondly of a corner pub, a fire, and a nice book to read. Instead, she was huddled in her rain jacket before a fire eating instant oatmeal in the mist.

Actually, it wasn't such a bad morning after all.

Decidedly cheerful—good sex will do that to a body—Sasha smiled when Declan came back from where he'd gone to relieve himself and check the perimeter to make sure the magick still held.

"Maddox," Declan said, nodding once briskly at Maddox.

"Declan," Maddox said, returning the nod stiffly.

Sasha remembered what she'd seen just before she'd gone under last night. "Are you two fighting?" she demanded.

"Just a difference of opinions," Maddox said, his nose about as high in the air as it could get.

"No, not a matter of differences. You were right and I'm sorry," Declan said, offering his hand.

Sasha almost beamed at him. There was nothing more attractive than a man who knew how to apologize when he was wrong—though from what she'd heard, she wasn't certain Declan had even been in the wrong. But it mattered little so long as there was peace among the group.

"Apology accepted. And I'm sorry for shoving you. I get a little protective of Sasha sometimes," Maddox said, shaking Declan's hand.

"As do I," Declan said, smiling and taking the bowl Bianca offered him.

"Well, now that we're all one big happy family again, what should we do today? Sasha thinks we should go look at the lighthouse during the day. But we were discussing things and we both agree that it doesn't make much sense to continue our stay at the castle. The Domnua know where we are now and will just set up watch until they find a weak point again."

"I think they'll find us anywhere we go," Maddox said, pointing with his spoon.

Declan sat next to Sasha, slightly behind her and leaning into her so that his bulk blocked the majority of the wind and mist for her. She leaned into his warmth, craving his nearness in a way that she wasn't yet certain she was comfortable with.

"We keep moving then. It will make me feel more comfortable as currently I feel like we are too vulnerable," Declan said.

"I think we need to move on. I'm not sure why we were brought here yet, but my gut says to keep going." Sasha looked at Bianca, who had raised an eyebrow and was motioning her head at Declan. "What?"

"Um, well, maybe you had to come here to, you know," Bianca said, nodding at the two of them again.

"To boink?" Sasha said, and Bianca burst out laughing.

"Who even says that? What are you, a thirteen-year-old boy?" Maddox said, rolling his eyes at Sasha.

"What? It's a technical term," Sasha said but grinned around her bite of oatmeal. No use hiding anything from these three anyway, so they might as well discuss it.

"I'm just saying… what if we were led here so that Sasha and Declan could realize they love each other? Then that is like a key that opens the next level," Bianca said.

Sasha choked on her oatmeal, coughing and sputtering as Declan pounded her back. She waved a hand in front of her face, brushing away the tears that clouded her eyes from coughing, and drew a shuddering breath. "I think we need to slow down a bit. No need to be throwing the L-word around all careless-like," Sasha said, clearing her throat and looking anywhere but at Declan.

"I mean… am I the only one that sees this?" Bianca looked around at the group, and Seamus smiled at her while Maddox gave a quick nod.

"I agree there may be some truth to this," Declan said, shocking Sasha into looking up at him.

"You love me?" she said, stunned that he was not shying away from this conversation.

His eyes crinkled at the corners and his face warmed as he looked down at her. "Aye, I do. What did you think this all was for? I wouldn't have said you were my destiny if you were just a woman I'd casually date and dismiss after a night or two. Look around at what we are doing. Where we are. The centuries of myths and legends that have led us here. The years I've watched you, protected you, claimed you as mine in my head. The years I had to watch you with other men – the wrong men – and still protect you anyway. Did you think this was anything less than love?"

Sasha's mouth was hanging open by the end of his statement – not only because it was the longest she had heard him talk, as he was typically a man of few words, but also because she could read the absolute truth behind his words. A warm glow filled her and for once she felt entirely safe with a man.

"I… I suppose that would make sense," Sasha said lamely, her fingers tapping on her leg as she thought about her response. "It's just that… for me this is all so new. And I haven't known you that long. It may take me a little longer to wrap my head and my heart around this all."

Declan held her eyes for a moment and in them was no censure – only understanding. "You take all the time you need, my love. I already know what I need to know," he said, leaning over and brushing a soft kiss over her lips before returning to his oatmeal.

Sasha was surprised to find herself just a little annoyed at his statement. Shouldn't she be the one to know how she felt? What made him think he knew? Annoyed, and frustrated at having her innermost demons and emotions continually exposed to the group, she stood. It wasn't easy walking around like a raw exposed nerve all the time.

"I'd like to go to the lighthouse after I use what passes for a bathroom around here. I think we should look for any other clues and then move on. Especially because it looks like heavier rain is going to move in."

With that, she turned her back on the group and faced into the rain, her heart beating a staccato beat in her chest while she kept her mind focused on the end goal.

Find the sword and go back to life as normal.

# CHAPTER 40

They climbed the stairs of the lighthouse, taking their time, this time with flashlights, and calling back to each other whenever a broken step appeared or a loose bolt was apparent. Sasha was still niggling over Declan's declaration of love, so she missed a step and almost went down, but he caught her – strong and steady behind her. Would it always be this way? Him there to catch her?

Sasha needed to come to terms with the fact that it already had always been this way. The only difference was that now she was included. It was like pulling back a curtain to reveal a secondary cast of characters in her life that she'd had no knowledge of. It was disconcerting, to say the least. It should have come as no surprise to anyone that she wasn't quite ready to drop the L-word yet.

"This is cool," Bianca exclaimed from the top, and soon they all crowded into the circular room.

The flame from yesterday had now died out, though it seemed to Sasha that another one had been ignited in her heart. Heat flushed her as she thought about Declan taking her against the wall, her body melded to his. Declan turned and flashed a knowing grin at her, and she jumped and turned away to begin to examine the room.

"It's fairly standard, for the century it was built in," Seamus said as they began to examine the stones, peeking through the window slots to look at different viewpoints.

"The view is phenomenal," Sasha sighed and leaned against one sliver of window that showed the ocean, uninterrupted for miles but for a moody seagull swooping in the misting rain. Though the weather was melancholy, there was something about the seagull that calmed her. There had been a battle raging on these very shores the night before, yet in the morning, the birds still flew and the rain still fell. Wars were waged, battles won and lost, and the world moved on. The continuity of it was a blessing.

Sasha smiled and turned, crossing her arms as she looked at her friends, the people who had now become her family. She looked up and murmured a silent 'thank you' to the Goddess.

And froze.

"Hey, is that a placard?" Sasha asked, pointed to a small metal square, bolted to the wall, far above their heads where the roof rounded to its peak.

"Good eye, Sash," Seamus said.

She gasped as he scaled the wall, nimble as a monkey, and peered at the square. Holding on with one hand, he brushed at the rust for a moment until he could see.

"Get anything?" Declan asked.

"There, but for the grace of God, go I," Seamus said, and dropped lightly back to his feet.

Sasha thought it was interesting that she had just been thinking about the circle of life, the ebb and flow of good and bad, and here was a quote that echoed the luck and misfortune of humanity.

"Grace's Cove!" Bianca said immediately.

Sasha looked at her in confusion. "Grace's Cove? I think I've heard of it. Village on the west coast?" she asked.

"It's near where we had our last battle and found the stone. The cove is enchanted. It's all very fantastic; I'll fill you in on the ride. But I'm certain this is where we need to go," Bianca said. Then she paused, her round face flushed as she held up a hand, and said, "Actually, it doesn't matter what I think. What do you think, Sasha? Does Grace's Cove feel right?"

"This was one of Grace O'Malley's castles," Declan said from behind her.

"It was? That's amazing. I have nothing but respect for Grace O'Malley. The original tough-as-nails woman. Did you know she gave birth at sea? And then went into battle? And women today talk about having perfect birth plans. Please. Grace O'Malley would laugh in their faces," Bianca pattered on behind her, but Sasha tuned her out and turned to look back at the lonely gull swooping above the crashing waves.

When it dove into the water and snatched a fish, the fish dangling from its mouth for a moment before meeting its death, Sasha nodded once.

*There but for the grace of God go I.*

# CHAPTER 41

"*I* love Grace's Cove. Once we kick Domnua butt, I want to spend a couple weeks there just puttering around in the shops, going for hikes along the coast, and maybe even spending time in the cove – if the cove will let me." Bianca chattered away and Sasha had half-listened as she twisted the quote around in her head once more.

"Wait, what? Why wouldn't the cove let you go there?"

"Oh, well, it's just the most romantic and melodramatic story ever," Bianca sighed and held her hand to her heart. "Romantic in an abstract way, you get me? Not like love-romantic. But Grace O'Malley chose to end her life in the cove, as she was very sick. And the night she walked into the water – blood sacrifice, strong magick – she enchanted the cove. Her daughter was there and gave birth on the beach that very night – double blood magick – and imbued the bloodline with extra special gifts. Now the cove basically doesn't let anyone in if they don't have O'Malley blood."

"Wait, like fairy magick? And how does it stop the people from getting in?" Sasha snorted out a laugh. "Like, is there a bouncer? Do they club people?"

Bianca turned and looked at her with a very serious look on her pert face.

"The water swallows them as soon as they get to the beach. It's not pretty. Nobody in the village will go there. They claim it's because there's a dangerous undertow, but everybody who lives there knows differently. They won't speak of it."

"Wow, that's kind of intense. So that's where the sword is? In a cove that will swallow us whole? Awesome," Sasha muttered. Declan reached up and wrapped an arm around her shoulder, tugging her in for a hug.

"Maybe not at the cove. But we can see how we feel once we get to town. Plus, maybe we'll find Fiona. Or we can always stop at Cait's pub. She was awesome and outfitted us for our hike to battle."

"Tell me how that went down," Sasha asked, and spent the rest of the drive listening to Bianca's engaging reenactment of the great battle that Clare had undertaken to secure the stone. Bianca was an excellent storyteller, but it also made Sasha realize that the end of this would not go easily.

"No chance I'm just going to trip over the sword, is there?" Sasha finally asked, a growing sense of dread creeping up her shoulders.

"Not likely. But you'll figure it out. I have faith," Bianca said, her endless optimism soothing Sasha a bit.

"How can you be sure?" Sasha asked.

"Because I believe in fairytale endings," Bianca smiled over her shoulder.

And that was that, Sasha thought as they followed a road that curved along a cliff, one side filled with sleepy sodden hills, the other sullen gray water. She wished she could share Bianca's easy belief in happy endings. Unfortunately, Sasha was far more pragmatic than that. Perhaps she was a realist, or perhaps she was a pessimist, but either way, she'd seen enough to know that fairytale endings were more the oddity than the usual. But nonetheless, it was sweet of Bianca, and her never-ending cheerfulness even in the face of battle was something Sasha could believe in and rely upon.

"Do you just want to go to the cove? Or should we go to town first?" Seamus asked, looking at Bianca.

"I think we go to the cove. Not that the town isn't darling, but I don't know. I don't see the Sword of Light appearing in the middle of Gallagher's Pub, you know?" Bianca said.

Sasha agreed with her. "The cove, first, I think."

Seamus directed the car down a road that skirted a small village tucked into the foothills of a beautiful bay. Looking almost like a green Christmas tree decorated with colorful ornaments, the village was absolutely charming, each store and house painted a different bright color, and colorful flags strung up in streamers over the streets.

Sasha could indeed see why Bianca would want to spend a few weeks here. "It's charming."

"It really is. I love how each building has a different design, or different windows, big doors, little doors, lace curtains in one window, stained glass in another. Pottery studios, bookstores, little bakeries…" Bianca sighed and clutched her hands to her chest. "It isn't that I don't love

Dublin and big city life, but isn't there just something about a beautiful village tucked on the water that calls to your heart?"

"Aye, it's lovely," Maddox agreed. "Though I'm sure every teenage boy and girl in town hates it and is dying to see the bright lights of the big city."

"Ah, teenage angst," Bianca chuckled. "I came from a small town, so I knew it well. There wasn't much to do but get ourselves into trouble. For the most part, I kept to my studies and worked until I could get into Dubs and move on."

"You weren't a troublemaker?" Seamus teased as he turned onto a smaller one-lane road that began to wind along the cliffs, which looked dangerously steep in Sasha's estimation.

"I've always been a good girl," Bianca said, fluttering her eyelashes at Seamus.

"Not that good," Seamus said, sending her a saucy wink.

Sasha smiled broadly at the both of them. Even in the face of danger, in the face of death, in the face of battle – they faced each other with love.

That was certainly something to think about.

The sea stretched before them, unmarred by land, almost the same shade of gray as the ominous clouds that hung low in the horizon. More birds swooped here, the rain doing little to deter them from their daily meal, and the waves crashed dangerously upon jagged rocks that jutted up from the shoreline. The ocean never failed to make Sasha feel but like a minuscule speck of nothingness in a web of something so much greater. Who was she to think she was something in this world? How was she going to impact the world or change it for the better?

Sasha leaned back and watched Seamus navigate a particularly dicey turn in the road. It seemed she was going to impact the world – if she found the sword, that is. And in the history of time nobody would know what she had done for humanity. Was she okay with that? Did she need the accolades? Or would she be content knowing she had quietly effected massive change?

Realizing that the accolades didn't matter, but the change did, Sasha vowed to herself that, no matter what awful or uncomfortable situation she was thrown into in order to find this damn sword, she'd weather it.

Because people like Bianca and Seamus deserved a world they could smile in.

# CHAPTER 42

"Fiona!" Bianca exclaimed as they bumped down a gravel lane, having turned off from the main road. A woman, easily eighty years old if a day, perched casually on a stone wall, a dog at her side.

It could have been a sunny day in spring for the way the woman was casually sitting in the rain, a bright smile on her face, her dog's tongue lolling happily out of its mouth by her side. A bright red rain slicker mostly covered her white hair, and her pants were tucked into serviceable Wellies. She waved a hello to stop them.

"Hi, Fiona," Bianca called out of the window she rolled down.

"Come to my house for a cup of tea and a chat. No need to go to the cove on a grumpy day like today," Fiona said easily, whistling for her dog. "Ronan, home." The dog raced like a bullet across the wet field, his ears streaming behind him, toward a stone cottage that sat a ways up the lane.

"Do you want a ride?" Bianca asked.

Fiona laughed. "No, child. Go on. John's up there. I'll be along. Just a few more herbs to gather."

Gathering herbs in the rain, Sasha thought, and shook her head. There were so many other ways to spend a rainy day. A flash of her and Declan tangled in bed, with the rain pouring outside, had her stomach flipping over in knots. She pushed the thought away and instead focused on the cheerful cottage they were pulling up to.

A man, easily the same age as Fiona, crouched by the door and toweled off Ronan, who danced in anticipation of going inside. The cottage was made of stone, with pretty little red flower boxes and a bright door. Turning her head, Sasha gasped.

"You can't beat the view," she said, and Bianca turned and nodded at her.

"Isn't it fabulous? It's like you're at the end of the world and everything drops away. Could you imagine waking up to this every day?"

Sasha could, though it went against her busy city-soul nature. But a few weeks out here? With nothing to do but wander the hills and dream out at the ocean? Yeah, she could see the appeal.

"Come in, come in," John—or so Sasha presumed—said, waving to them.

They all dashed from the car and past a beaming John through the door of the cottage. It opened to one big room. In the center stood a long table with benches on both sides, and behind it was a wall lined with shelves that left Sasha gaping. There had to be hundreds of bottles, glass jars, and jugs, all meticulously labeled. To the left, a country kitchen sink stood beneath a huge window that overlooked the water. To the right was an alcove with a few beautiful rocking chairs tucked into it, a peat-moss fireplace, and a delighted baby crawling across a beautifully woven rug of warm reds and blues.

"This is baby Grace. We have her for the weekend," John said, walking over to Grace, who demanded to be picked up. He brought her to his hip, and the baby clapped her hands, then surveyed the lot of them with eyes that were far too intelligent for a baby.

Declan whistled, long and low.

"You've got a real corker on your hands with that one, don't you," he said.

"Aye, she's a feisty lass, that's for sure," John agreed.

"There's more there, isn't there?" Seamus surmised, tilting his head at the baby. Grace tilted her head right back at him, making them all laugh.

"Aye, she's a touch of something more than all of us combined," Fiona said from the doorway, and baby Grace clapped her hands in enthusiasm when she saw Fiona.

Placing a basket with some herbs on the table, Fiona pointed at Grace.

"You just hold on, Grace. You know I've got to attend to my guests. I'll be back to teaching you in just a bit."

That baby understood every word Fiona said – Sasha would have sworn it. Grace scowled at Fiona first, and then daintily inclined her head at her, and Fiona chuckled.

"That one, I tell you. She's been nothing but a joy and a pain in our arses since the day she was born." Fiona winked at Grace, who just winked right back at her.

Oh yeah, something definitely different about that

baby, Sasha thought, and moved to the bench where Fiona gestured for them to sit.

"I'll just get tea on. Perhaps with a touch of the Irish on this fine day?" Fiona asked as they all settled in and finished introducing themselves to her and John.

"Gracie would like to sit with you," John said from over Sasha's shoulder, startling her.

"Oh, um, well, I'm not that great with…" Sasha trailed off as she found a baby deposited in her arms. She stared down into the sherry-brown eyes of this cherubic baby and thought, *"Please don't cry."*

Grace dimpled up at her, but did nothing other than bang her palms on the table.

"Don't you like children?" Fiona asked, putting a basket of warm scones in front of them, along with a crock of butter that Sasha wondered if she had churned herself. Passing out little plates, Fiona gestured for them to dig in.

"It's not that I don't like children. I just haven't had a lot of experience around them," Sasha admitted, gingerly bouncing Grace and hoping the baby didn't get mad at her.

"Do you want children?" Bianca asked, her face openly curious, and Sasha paused as she was reaching for a scone. "I'm sorry. That's rude of me."

"I don't want children. No," Sasha admitted and turned to see surprise quickly cross Declan's face. Ha! He said he loved her, but did he know that she wouldn't want a tradi-tional stay-at-home-mum lifestyle? See, maybe it wasn't really love for him either.

Baby Grace turned and put a tiny hand on Sasha's cheek, her pretty eyes trained on Sasha's.

*Love.*

Sasha started. Had the baby just spoken to her telepathically, or was she losing her mind? See, Sasha chided herself, you open yourself to magick and then you start thinking you see it everywhere. The baby patted her cheek one more time.

*Love. Trust it.*

"Is she talking to you? I swear she just likes getting in everyone's minds. This one is going to give all of us a run for our money," Fiona chuckled. "Don't you let her tell you anything you aren't ready to hear, Sasha. You're allowed to not want to have children. Not everyone is interested in being a mother and there is nothing wrong with that. Now you let her be, Gracie." Fiona plucked a laughing Grace from Sasha's lap and went to rock her at the end of the table.

"She can talk to you like that?" Bianca asked, her eyes wide.

"I'm pretty certain she's going to be able to do whatever she feels like doing," Fiona said, chuckling again.

Bianca reached out to pretend high-five the baby. "Way to be awesome, little one." The whole table laughed when Grace slapped her palm against Bianca's in delight.

"So, the sword," Fiona said, rocking Grace and leveling her eyes on Sasha. "Fill me in thus far."

"I'll take that. I like to tell stories," Bianca said cheerfully. "And by the way, these blueberry scones are to die for. So, here is what we know…"

Sasha zoned out for a moment as she spread butter on her warm scone, watching it melt in rivulets, her mind on what Baby Grace had told her. Was there a clue in Grace's Cove about love?

*There but for the grace of God go I.*

"How are you feeling?" Declan asked, nudging her with his leg.

She looked up at him. "I'm confused. I feel like everyone is right – I hold the answer. But I don't know what that is, or how I could just suddenly materialize a sword in front of me by clicking a locked door inside my mind open, you know?"

"Sure, I understand. But maybe you're being too hard on yourself. Maybe you just need to trust that it will all unfold as it needs to."

She wondered if his words had more meaning for her, and the thought made her a bit skittish. Would she be able to live up to his expectations? Was she even worthy of his love? Frustrated, she tore off a piece of scone and shoved it in her mouth, turning back when her name was spoken.

"I'm sorry, what was that?"

"Have you given any other thought to the clue about going where the light always shines?" Fiona asked, her eyes sparkling with warmth.

"The only other thing that popped into my head was a sundial. But that doesn't really make sense because it isn't lit up at night or if it's cloudy, that kind of thing."

"Ah, methinks you are thinking too literally. You need to play fast and loose with these clues, as the fae certainly like to do so with the rules." Fiona regarded the fae at the table sternly, and they seemed to shrink a little under her gaze.

"The Domnua more so than us," Seamus protested.

"There's a sundial not far from here. An ancient one, used to mark the passage of days, and even weeks or months. It's but a circle of stones with a prominent altar in the middle. The altar was used for worship, as well as casting shadows as the sun made its path. Keep in mind that a shadow will almost always fall on a sundial – no matter in moonlight or sunlight. I'd seriously consider this as a spot to go investigate. It's on holy ground, so there's no reason that magick won't be strong there," Fiona said evenly.

Sasha looked at her in shock. "I was right?" Sasha squeaked.

"Maybe, maybe not. But if that is what your first instinct was, then I suggest you'd better investigate. Though I'd wait until morning. Night falls soon and this rain won't let up for hours yet."

"May we camp on your land?" Declan asked politely, and Fiona looked at him in horror.

"Camping? In this weather? No, you'll be staying at Keelin and Flynn's house, just over the way there. They're on a little holiday, which is why we're watching this wee one. You're free to use their house as your own; they've plenty of guest rooms. I've called over to their stable hand already, when I woke this morning and knew you were coming. The fire should be stoked and going."

"How'd you know we were coming?" Bianca asked, and both Fiona and the baby looked at her with expressions akin to pity.

"Whoops, sorry. Got it," Bianca said, pointing a finger at her head.

"John will take you over while I attempt to get this one fed. The pantry should be stocked, but if nothing else, there are a few frozen pizzas in the freezer. Though it goes against everything I believe in, I don't think I'll be able to cook you dinner this night," Fiona said.

"Pizza is fine. We're all pretty exhausted after the last few days. I'm sure we'll have an early evening," Maddox said easily and stood. "Thank you for the scones and the words of guidance."

"Will you be safe? If the Domnua follow us here?" It was something Sasha didn't think she'd be able to handle – not this sweet old couple and otherworldly baby. They needed peace, not war on their front doorstep.

"Aye, we're well protected. Have no fear for us. We're more powerful than you'll ever know," Fiona said, her tone fearsome and the light of a warrior in her eyes.

So much for sweet old woman, Sasha thought, almost snorting out a laugh. She wouldn't wish Fiona on her worst enemy.

"In that case, we'll let you know what we find at the sundial tomorrow," Declan said, and they all stood, shaking hands and hugging as they filed out.

Fiona stopped Sasha at the door, baby Grace once more reaching up to touch her cheek.

*Trust.*

Sasha met Fiona's eyes and Fiona only nodded once before turning away to coo to the baby.

# CHAPTER 43

The farmhouse John directed them to was anything but the quaint farmhouse she had been expecting after seeing Fiona's stone cottage. Sasha would describe this more as a spread. The main house itself was large, with several wings jutting off from the core, and there were myriad outbuildings and stables scattered through the hills. A few dogs ran up to the car as they drove up, wagging their tails in excitement at the visitors.

"You're fine to just go on in. Best of luck to you. Please call us for anything – and I do mean anything," John said pointedly before rolling the window of his truck back up and honking lightly to nudge the dogs out of the way. Then he meandered his way back up the hill toward the cottage.

"Real beds!" Bianca bounced in her seat.

Sasha slanted her a look. "You slept on the ground for one night."

"One night too many. My neck hurts," Bianca said, getting out to round the car and start carrying supplies in.

In a matter of minutes they'd hauled everything inside the house, and began exploring, finding the guest wing fairly easily.

"I like this one," Sasha decided, tugging on her braid as she peeked into a pretty room with a large bed done up in navy and green plaid, with a dark wood headboard, and a wall of windows with a door that faced the stormy sea.

"Works for me," Declan said, and walked in to sling his bag on the bed.

"Oh," Sasha said, not having considered the fact that they might share a bed together.

"Get used to it," Declan said, walking over to put a finger under her chin. Lifting her face, he brushed a kiss over her mouth before heading down the hallway to check out the rest of the house.

"How is it so easy for him?" Sasha grumbled, and pulled out her toiletries. Locating the attached bath, she treated herself to a warm steamy shower.

It was so interesting to her how, days ago, Declan had been rejecting her and insisting that it would compromise the mission if he were to detour from the path he had set for himself. It was as if once he had accepted the inevitable, he was able to just slide into easy couple-mode with her.

Sasha flinched at the word 'couple.' Nothing about being part of a couple brought good memories to her, though she knew it wasn't fair to project her past feelings about relationships onto Declan.

Different man. Different expectations.

Sasha toweled off and made use of the lotion by the sink,

which smelled faintly of vanilla, and braided her towel-dried hair back from her face. Forgoing makeup, as she had little use for the stuff anyway, she pulled on comfy leggings and an oversized plaid shirt before making her way down to where she could hear voices at the center of the house.

"You showered!" Bianca accused her, standing by the kitchen table pouring a glass of wine.

"Duh," Sasha said.

Bianca glowered at her. "That's what I am going to go do right now. And I'm taking my glass of wine with me," Bianca huffed, disappearing from the room. Seamus glanced at the door a few times before Maddox finally sighed.

"Well? Go take your shower together, you two love-birds. I'm sure we can manage putting frozen pizzas in the oven." Seamus was gone from the room before Maddox was done speaking.

"If there really was a goddess, she'd grant me a beautiful man as a gift for my servitude," Maddox complained and Sasha went over to hug him.

"You've had many a man, many a night, if I recall. You can get anyone you want."

"True, 'tis true. I'm just being bitchy," Maddox laughed up at her.

"So what are we thinking? Pizza out by that gorgeous fireplace I spotted in the living room? Maybe some sundial research? Plan of action?" Sasha asked, pouring herself a glass of the red wine.

"Yes, to all of the above. The oven's preheating and there are several varieties of pizza in the freezer. Shouldn't be all that long before we have food. Why don't you go out by the fire now?" Declan said.

Sasha and Maddox both stood at once. "That room is too beautiful to ignore," Maddox said as they walked down a hallway peppered with pictures of a smiling baby Grace, toward where a huge stone fireplace dominated a room full of windows that opened out to the water. It was just past twilight now, but Sasha imagined the view was world-class when the sun was shining.

As promised, the fire was crackling cheerfully and firewood was stacked in the alcove next to the fireplace. Shelves of books lined the walls, and deep-seated couches and armchairs scattered around the room, all tossed with softly woven throws.

"I could spend a week here reading and be happy as a clam," Sasha decided, curling up in the corner of one of the couches and pulling a throw onto her lap. Just as she suspected, it was soft as a kitten's fur.

Maddox settled next to her, his eyes searching her face.

"You doing okay, sugar? I'm worried about you," Maddox said, glancing over his shoulder to make sure they were still alone.

"I'm doing the best I can." Sasha shrugged a shoulder. "It's just been a lot. Especially the whole 'having to examine every one of my personal insecurities' part of this. I kind of feel like I'm walking around as an exposed nerve right now."

"When was the last time you let yourself feel all these feelings?" Maddox countered, and Sasha paused to think about it.

"To be honest? I don't know. I think I've been on

autopilot for quite a while now. It's been easier to run a business and focus on that than it has to delve too deeply into any personal stuff," Sasha admitted, taking a sip of her wine and turning to look into the fire.

"Ah, well. The universe has a way of forcing us to address things – even when we don't think we are ready. But typically, we are." Maddox nodded sagely.

Sasha slanted him a look. "I'd say the universe has gone above and beyond in forcing me to address things in this particular situation," Sasha said.

Maddox laughed and patted her leg. "I always told you that you were special, sugar."

# CHAPTER 44

$\mathcal{B}$y the time they went to bed, Sasha was half-buzzed on wine and drowsy from the emotional rollercoaster of the past week. The evening had been fun, cozied up in front of the fire, eating pizza and tossing out theories on everything from sundials to the Sword of Light being like a lightsaber from Star Wars.

Sasha chuckled as she slid into bed, still in her leggings and flannel. Declan stepped out of the bathroom, a towel slung low on his hips, his chest still damp from his shower, and Sasha forgot what she had been laughing about.

"Something funny?"

"Um," Sasha said.

Very articulate, she chided herself, and bit her lower lip as Declan put his arms above him on the doorframe and leaned just a little, his muscles rippling, making her mind fuzz around the edges and lust slide low and deep inside her.

"Ah," Declan said, reading her correctly and dropping

the towel. Sasha gulped and buried herself further under the covers as Declan crawled onto the bed, caging her face in his hands as he took her under with his kiss.

"It seems you have some walls up here," Declan said, coming up from the kiss and tugging lightly at the blanket. She wondered briefly if he meant metaphorically, and then shivered as he stripped the blanket down and began unbuttoning her flannel. It did not take him long to storm the walls and soon after, Sasha gasped as he brought her over the cliff and into a bliss that she'd not known with any other man.

"It seems you're good at breaking past my walls," Sasha admitted when they were curled together, her head on his chest, his hand lightly stroking her back.

"I'm working on it. The physical is only one aspect of this though," Declan said, his voice sleepy. "But I'm not going anywhere and I won't give up until I've scaled the walls. I get why you've put them up. Nobody is judging you for it. I'm a patient man, and you're worth fighting for."

Sasha blinked back the tears that had slipped into her eyes at his unexpected words. She opened her mouth to respond but realized that Declan's breathing had changed, and he let out a soft snore, indicating he'd fallen asleep. She stayed there, curled to his warmth, and blinked back the flood of tears that threatened.

Nobody had ever once promised to stay by her side.

And goddess help her, she actually believed him.

# CHAPTER 45

*S*asha blinked awake, uncertain whether a noise had woken her, knowing only that she'd heard a voice in her head telling her she must go.

She must go now.

Glancing over at Declan, still snoring lightly, she watched his breath and saw that he was in a very deep sleep. Sliding from beneath the covers, she bent to pick up her clothes and, padding naked from the room, walked down the hallway to the kitchen where she quickly put on her clothes and her boots, grabbed a cap to pull down over her braid, and found herself stumbling over the wet grass in but a few moments.

She wasn't sure what had compelled her from her sleep – but one thing she was absolutely certain of was that she needed to go to this sundial on her own.

This was her burden to carry, and nobody else's.

The rain had abated, but the ground was soggy beneath Sasha's feet as she trudged across the field, following the slope of the hill, instinctively knowing where she needed to go. The sun had yet to rise, and the predawn light lent an unearthly glow to her surroundings. She finally came upon a single small path, like one the saints had once walked in pilgrimage, which she too would follow to find the truth.

The path led for a ways along a hill until it dipped low and out toward a large ledge that jutted out toward the sea. She was out of sight of the house now, and it was simply her, the sky above, and the sea below. In this moment, she would need to follow her gut instincts.

Finding the circle of stones was easy enough, as they all but pulsed with energy for her. Sasha walked slowly up the path until she stood just outside the round circle of stones, the pillar in the middle seeming to glow even brighter than the other stones. Standing there, she allowed herself to just be, with no expectations other than to feel the pulse of the universe, the natural ebb and flow of the wind and the waves, and to try to connect to it deep within her soul.

She wasn't the least bit prepared for it when Aaron stepped from behind the pillar, the same snarky grin he'd always worn lighting his face as he ran his gaze over her.

"Would it kill you to wear makeup once in a while?" Aaron asked, his legs braced wide, his arms crossed over his chest. He was as handsome as he'd ever been, with dark hair curling beneath a wool cap, and his flashing blue eyes were trained on hers. She watched him carefully to make sure she wasn't losing her mind – or still in a dream.

"Why in the world would I wear makeup when I am out for a morning hike?" Sasha asked, moving a bit to try to start circling the stones. Her hand, clutching the dagger, was concealed by the long loose arms of the oversized flannel shirt she still wore.

"It wouldn't kill you to try and make yourself look nicer. Maybe I wouldn't have left you if you'd cleaned yourself up once in a while." Aaron shook his head, letting out a derisive laugh as he moved closer to her.

"I think I look just fine," Sasha said evenly, keeping her eyes trained on him, though she couldn't help feel the sting of his words.

"And don't get me started on your poor performance in bed. Ever hear of wearing lingerie once in a while?" Aaron shook his head and Sasha flashed to Declan, peeling the covers off of her earlier that night and unbuttoning her flannel. Despite herself, she felt shame creep in.

The minute it did, Aaron leaped, grabbing her arm. In a flash they were transported from the circle, Sasha screaming at him to let her go.

"Oh hush. Nobody can hear you anyway." Aaron laughed, long and loud, as he held her from behind, one arm wrapped around her throat.

"Where are we?" Sasha asked, then gasped once more as she realized they'd landed in her parents' kitchen. It was like they were there, but nobody could see them.

"Mom!" Sasha called, and Aaron laughed again.

"They can't actually hear you. We're just here to have a quick listen. Now, hush up."

He clamped his hand over her mouth, and Sasha had no choice but to listen.

"Why is she always a problem? It's constant drama with her," her mother said to her father, who nodded in agreement, pointing a fork full of spaghetti across the table.

"Right? I just wish things would go smoothly for once. If only she'd just gone to Uni and met a nice boy and settled down, things would be fine. But it's always something with her," her father complained.

"That's why I'm your favorite, right?" Her sister, Chelsea, whom she hadn't seen in years, laughed across the table at them.

"Naturally. You've never given us issues. To this day, I still wish we'd never taken Sasha in. She's caused us nothing but trouble and torment," her mother said.

Sasha felt the knife of pain twist low and deep in her gut. As she'd always known, her parents favored Chelsea and had never really wanted her. It had been confirmed for her several times on this journey, so it was best that she just learn to let things go in her head.

"Speaking of Chelsea," Aaron whispered in her ear, laughing as they left the room, somehow being transported elsewhere. Sasha felt herself gag against Aaron's hand.

They were in the bedroom of the apartment she had shared with Aaron, the framed picture of them smiling in front of the Eiffel Tower hanging over the bed. Except instead of her lying in bed with Aaron, as it should have been, it was her sister Chelsea. Sasha blinked back tears as Chelsea wound her arms around Aaron's neck, leaning in to kiss and nuzzle him.

When they began to touch each other more intimately, Sasha simply closed her eyes, refusing to look.

"Don't you see, Sasha? You've never been good enough," Aaron laughed.

Sasha felt the little sucking pull of them being whooshed away elsewhere, and this time she just kept her eyes closed, her entire body vibrating with anger, shame clinging to her like a silky second skin as she waited for whatever was next.

Hearing Declan's voice was not what she expected.

Her eyes popped open despite herself, and this time the tears ran down her cheeks as she watched Declan laugh with his arm around a smiling blonde-haired woman. They sat outside at a little trattoria, enjoying a bottle of wine. Declan leaned over to brush a kiss over the woman's lips, the same way he had done to her earlier that night, and the blonde twinkled up at him.

"See? Even he lies. When will you understand, Sasha? You'll never be good enough. Stop wishing for more," Aaron said, once again whisking them away until they stood inside her very own gallery, though things had changed.

And then she saw herself.

She'd changed. Gray shot through her hair, and her shoulders had slumped slightly. She stood speaking harshly with a customer before the customer stormed out. Striding across the room, the older version of her slammed the door and locked it, her face set in hard lines as she walked back to her desk and slammed a book down on it. Dropping into her chair, she crossed her arms and stared at the wall, her face a mask of rage.

No, Sasha thought. I don't want that to be me. I will never be that bitter or closed off.

Or alone.

*There but for the grace of God go I.*

In seconds, Aaron brought her back to the circle, dancing around her in laughter as the tears ran in rivulets down her face, her entire body shaking with shame and anger, her every sadness exposed.

She lifted her head.

$\mathcal{T}$rust.

Baby Grace had thrust that word deep into her head, along with the word love. Trust love. Sasha now knew what she meant. As she watched Aaron dance in glee at her sadness, she allowed trust to fill her heart.

She allowed love to flow into all the aching crevices of her body until it filled her about to bursting.

Her parents loved her. She knew that – even though things had not always been perfect. But no family was perfect, and they'd done the best they could with a difficult and awkward child who was not entirely of this realm.

Her sister was just fine, happy in her marriage with her two babies – there was no way she'd ever look twice at Aaron.

And as for Declan – well, he'd protected her for his entire life. He'd promised her he'd keep standing by her side, would break through her walls, and was always going to be there for her. His destiny, he'd said. And her gut told her it was so.

As did her heart.

No, she wouldn't grow old and bitter and shut out the love that was given to her. She had wonderful friends, a nice family, and an amazing man who wanted to stand with her for her lifetime.

Trust.

And so Sasha met Aaron's eyes dead on.

He stopped dancing, cocking his head in confusion at her.

Sasha stepped into the circle, walking forward until she stood at the pillar. Silence fell around them, and she could no longer even hear the waves crashing or the call of the gull as it swooped over the water.

"I forgive you," Sasha said, looking into Aaron's eyes as his mouth fell open.

The sword materialized instantly in the pillar before her, just as the sun broke the horizon, its rays lancing across the water to highlight the stone.

Without a second's thought, Sasha pulled the sword from the stone and plunged it through Aaron's heart.

She knew it wasn't really Aaron she was killing, but her own self-doubts. And as the Domnua that had masqueraded as Aaron melted in a silvery puddle to the earth below them, so too did her insecurities, and Sasha stepped into her own power.

She stood there, trembling with the force of the incredible gift she'd been given, before she finally heard the cries behind her. Turning, she saw her friends, along with Fiona, John, and baby Grace, standing outside the wall, pounding on an invisible barrier.

And Declan, his heart in his face, his hands pressed to the barrier, waiting.

Waiting for her to choose him.

She stepped through the thin membrane of magick, and was immediately swamped, everyone trying to hug her at once, while Declan stood back, his face a mask.

"Hold this," Sasha said, handing the sword to Fiona, who took it reverently, running her hands over the jeweled hilt as Sasha pushed through to stand before Declan.

"Hey," she said softly, looking up into his beautiful eyes, wanting nothing more than to jump into his arms, but sensing she had to tread carefully here.

"You left. Without me," Declan bit out, looking away and then back down at her, his fists clenched at his sides.

"I had to. I had to do this on my own. It was the only way," Sasha said softly.

"I'm supposed to protect you. I can't do that if you just leave me," Declan said, still visibly angry.

"I had no choice. Not in this matter. But I do now. And I choose you. I love you, Declan. For life. My destiny," Sasha reached up and placed her hand over where his heart beat fast in his chest. "My heart. I'm sorry I had to leave like that, but this is what was needed so I could come to you freely."

Declan clasped a hand over hers, taking a long moment to read what he needed from her eyes before sweeping her into his arms, his lips finding hers and sealing their promise to each other.

Baby Grace laughed and clapped in the background, which caused the entire group to laugh. Sasha turned to look at them, her face pressed to Declan's chest as Fiona held the sword to the sun and the light captured it in all its glory.

"We're free now, you and me," Sasha whispered to Declan and he pressed a kiss to the top of her head.

# EPILOGUE

"*W*hy do we have to go to the cove again?"
Sasha asked, feeling just a bit grumpy.
She'd just had this epic life-changing experience and all
she wanted to do was crawl into bed with Declan and pull
the covers over her head for days.

"Because you have to take the sword somewhere, duh.
It's the Sword of freaking Light!" Bianca exclaimed. "You
can't just, like, put it on the kitchen counter and deal with
it later."

"Your friend makes an excellent point. To the cove we
go," Fiona laughed.

And so Sasha found herself, walking hand-in-hand
with Declan, at the first brush of dawn across the
extraordinary cliffs that jutted proudly out into the sea,
cradling a perfect half circle of beach far below them.
They stopped at the top of a path that zigzagged its way
down to the untouched shore below them.

"You go on. We'll watch from above. Tell the Goddess

hello for me," Fiona said and Bianca paused to look back at her.

"Need we do any ritual? Or present a gift or anything?" Bianca asked.

Baby Grace shook her head no and Fiona laughed again. "I think the Sword of Light is gift enough, no?"

"I suppose as gifts go, it's quite good," Bianca conceded.

They wound their way down the path, the breeze just a light caress on their cheeks today, the water calm as they made their way to the beach.

"So this is the infamous enchanted beach?" Sasha asked once they'd stepped onto the sand. "I can see why Grace would want her final resting spot to be kept private here. It's quite stunning."

"Not as stunning as this creature," Declan murmured in her ear and then astonished her by dropping to his knees.

"Are you proposing?" Sasha asked, her hand at her heart, then jumped when a laugh sounded behind her, like a hundred bluebirds singing. Whirling around, she gaped at the vision before her.

Light seemed to shimmer and shift around the image of a woman, but an everywoman, so beautiful that she was never one shape or color. She was the all-powerful She – the essence of all – and Sasha found herself frozen to the spot in awe.

"Thank you for your sacrifices upon the way. We are indebted to you." Goddess Danu's voice, like rich wine, fell upon her and Sasha bowed her head.

"I am grateful that I was able to succeed in my mission," she stuttered.

"You'll have a blessed life for it. The sword?" Goddess Danu held out her hand and Sasha skittered forward, bowing awkwardly again as she placed the sword in the Goddess's hands. Danu smiled, running a hand down Sasha's cheek.

"You're more beautiful than you'll ever know. Never forget to live in love. It is the only true currency that matters in this world."

"I promise to remember," Sasha said, but Danu had already disappeared, leaving Sasha with her hand pressed to her cheek where the Goddess had just touched her.

"I swear, she could appear to me a million times and it would never get old," Bianca sprang up and did a little dance in the sand, her blonde pigtails bouncing. "She's freaking cool!"

Declan stood again and came to Sasha's side, looking down at her.

"Did you want me to be proposing then?"

"I mean – I guess, well – not like, *now*. But you know, seeing as you're my destiny and all... we should probably get married at some point," Sasha laughed, then gasped when he swept her into his arms.

"Look," Declan said, nuzzling at her ear and she turned to see a vibrantly glowing blue light shooting from the water. Sasha's eyes widened in surprise and she looked up to see Baby Grace clapping her hands in laughter.

"Is the baby doing that?"

"No, silly, the cove glows in the presence of true love. It's part of the enchantment," Bianca said, a goofy smile on her face.

Maddox had pulled a handkerchief out and pressed it to his nose. "I guess I've got a wedding to start planning."

"Enchanted, indeed," Declan said, sliding his lips over hers. "And I'm enchanted with you."

And for the first time, Sasha allowed herself to believe in the fairytale ending.

The Isle of Destiny Series, Book 3- Available now as an e-book, paperback or audiobook!

Sign up for information on new releases, free books, and fun giveaways at my website www.triciaomalley.com

---

The following is an excerpt from Spear Song

Book 3 in The Isle of Destiny Series

# CHAPTER 1

"*B*e still, mother, just now. Just for a moment, now. That's it, love, open your mouth," Lochlain crooned, tilting his mother's head back as he poured another elixir down her throat. It was the fifth carefully-curated potion he'd used just this day and, to his dismay, none of his tinctures were reversing the spell which was slowly murdering his mother from the inside out.

"May the lot of you rot forever in darkness, Domnua," Loch hissed, turning to pace the room as he raked a hand through dark hair that tumbled around a sharply angled face. His golden eyes all but glowed in rage as he continued to curse, his mind racing through the last of the magicks he could possibly perform to save his mother's life.

It had been three days since she'd encountered a Domnua on a foraging excursion deep in the isolated hills of western Ireland. As usual, she'd been harvesting ingredients for her spells that called for being plucked beneath the pale light of a new moon. It was also when the walls between the worlds were thin.

Too thin, as Loch had unfortunately learned. The infamous curse, which had kept the Danula safe and the Domnua banished to the underworld for centuries, was coming to its final days. As the clock ticked on, the Domnua flexed their power, slipping more easily into modern-day Ireland, shielding themselves as they began to enjoy the virtual playground humans provided for them.

The fae – both good and bad – could never resist the fallacies and dramas that came with the human condition. An extended lifespan could do that to a soul, causing the fae to be drawn to the resilient spirit of the humans, endlessly fascinated by watching both wars and love stories unfold.

Once the Domnua had begun to taste their freedom again, keeping them contained had been like trying to hold two hands over a fire hose – they practically poured through the thin veil that separated the worlds. Loch's mother should have known better; he'd warned her, hadn't he? Loch cursed again as his eyes strayed to where she lay on her side, curled beneath a blanket, the fire snapping away to provide additional warmth on this chilly spring day.

There'd been no reason to hurt her – aside from sending a message. Loch had heard tell of it across Ireland, whispered conversations in pubs and snippets of tales from travelers. The Domnua wanted to show they weren't scared, which meant trying to kill the innocents. And had his mother not been as high up in the fae world as she was – a venerable priestess at that – she'd be dead now. Her magick had saved her, but now Loch had to wonder if it was only prolonging a painful end. Coming to his knees at her side, he pressed a hand to her cheek.

"My mother, my heart, I will find your cure. This I promise." Loch pressed his lips to her forehead.

"My son. My heart. If I must go… I must go. My own fault." Her words trailed off, and Loch's heart skipped as he waited for her to take a staggered breath.

"'Tis not your fault, mother, 'tis the murdering Domnua. I will avenge this. But first, I must be off to find you help. I've exhausted my remedies."

"My child. My stubborn, beautiful son. You have such good in you. Don't let the dark win." Her words faded, and Loch wondered if there was a hidden meaning to them. He had no time to waste, though, and brushed his lips over her forehead once more, promising a swift return. Then he rushed from their home with but one destination in mind.

Loch raced through the mists of the early morning, which clung to the moody hedges and rolling hills that sheltered a town that was not known to mortal men. Any human passerby would simply see an expanse of barren hills, but if they were to attempt to climb or explore, they'd be met with a tangled hedge so impenetrable that they would be forced to turn back. His village of magickal people, the Danula, had a stronghold here – one of many scattered throughout Ireland. And far deeper within those hills was a sacred cave of such legend and enchantment that no fae dared go there, as the penalty was death.

Loch paused as he drew near. He felt the press of magick, the invisible barrier of the first ward that would alert to movement near the cave, and stopped just short of it. Reaching out with his extra senses, Loch began to track and find where the various wards and enchantments were. Reaching deep within to magicks he was sworn to never use, Loch began to invalidate and null the wards, spinning quickly through each boundary, firing off spells and magicks until he stood in front of the cave, his heart racing.

If he stepped through this door, his life would be forfeit.

But his mother would live.

Without a second thought, Loch pushed through the door and rushed to find the one thing he knew would save his mother – a bottle of sacred blood from the Goddess Danu herself. Not needing light to see – his eyes adjusted quickly – he raced through the rooms, assessing and discarding all the various treasures found there. Had he more time, he'd allow himself the joy of sifting through the beauty of what was a veritable Aladdin's cave, but every second counted.

Both for his own life and his mother's.

Loch drew to a stop, having rounded a narrow rocky outcropping to find what he sought: a blown glass bottle, twisted and turned in a gossamer-thin veil of faintly purple crystal, vines reaching toward petals containing a Celtic quaternary knot. The stopper itself was a ruby rose of purest red, mirroring the liquid it contained within.

For one infinitesimal moment, Loch's heart stopped as he allowed the sacred beauty of something only whispered about in legends to wash over him, before he shut his thoughts and his fears down. At this point, he was a warrior with one goal in mind – get the magick to his mother. Reaching out, he wrapped his hands around the bottle and tugged it gently from the stand on which it was nestled.

Instantly, light – a thousand times as bright as the stars – lit the room, blinding him, as the sound of the Mireesi, the goddess's avenging angels, raged through the cave, their sound as beautiful as it was painful. It ravaged through his head like millions of razor blades slicing his mind. Before the song made him lose his mind, as it was sure to do, Loch pulled out the last trick he had and vanished into thin air as the angelic warriors flooded the protected space – only to find an empty room with the most sacred of blood missing.

As their cries of despair rolled across the land, those in the village froze, knowing there was a breach, knowing that a death of one of their own was imminent. All eyes turned towards the hills, where a flood of amethyst warriors, winged beasts of the most glorious creation, rolled on molten waves as they poured from every crevice in the hills, madly searching for the one – the only fae in all of time – who had been powerful enough to breach their wards.

And to ensure his death was immediate.

**Audio, e-book & paperback!**
Available from Amazon

# ALSO BY TRICIA O'MALLEY

## THE ISLE OF DESTINY SERIES

**Stone Song**

**Sword Song**

**Spear Song**

**Sphere Song**

———

**A completed series in Kindle Unlimited.**

**Available in audio, e-book & paperback!**

"Love this series. I will read this multiple times. Keeps you on the edge of your seat. It has action, excitement and romance all in one series."

- Amazon Review

# THE ENCHANTED HIGHLANDS

**Wild Scottish Knight**

**Wild Scottish Love**

**Wild Scottish Rose**

---

"I love everything Tricia O'Malley has ever written and "Wild Scottish Knight" is no exception. The new setting for this magical journey is Scotland, the home of her new husband and soulmate. Tricia's love for her husbands country shows in every word she writes. I have always wanted to visit Scotland but have never had the time and money. Having read "Wild Scottish Knight" I feel I have begun to to experience Scotland in a way few see it. I am ready to go see Loren Brae, the castle and all its magical creatures, for myself. Tricia O'Malley makes the fantasy world of Loren Brae seem real enough to touch!"

-Amazon Review

**Available in audio, e-book, hardback, paperback and is included in your Kindle Unlimited subscription.**

THE WILDSONG SERIES

**Song of the Fae**

**Melody of Flame**

**Chorus of Ashes**

**Lyric of Wind**

---

"The magic of Fae is so believable. I read these books in one sitting and can't wait for the next one. These are books you will reread many times."

- Amazon Review

**A completed series in Kindle Unlimited.**

**Available in audio, e-book & paperback!**

## THE SIREN ISLAND SERIES

**Good Girl**

**Up to No Good**

**A Good Chance**

**Good Moon Rising**

**Too Good to Be True**

**A Good Soul**

**In Good Time**

———

**A completed series in Kindle Unlimited.**

**Available in audio, e-book & paperback!**

"Love her books and was excited for a totally new and different one! Once again, she did NOT disappoint! Magical in multiple ways and on multiple levels. Her writing style, while similar to that of Nora Roberts, kicks it up a notch!! I want to visit that island, stay in the B&B and meet the gals who run it! The characters are THAT real!!!" - Amazon Review

## THE ALTHEA ROSE SERIES

**One Tequila**

**Tequila for Two**

**Tequila Will Kill Ya (Novella)**

**Three Tequilas**

**Tequila Shots & Valentine Knots (Novella)**

**Tequila Four**

**A Fifth of Tequila**

**A Sixer of Tequila**

**Seven Deadly Tequilas**

**Eight Ways to Tequila**

**Tequila for Christmas (Novella)**

———

"Not my usual genre but couldn't resist the Florida Keys setting. I was hooked from the first page. A fun read with just the right amount of crazy! Will definitely follow this series."- Amazon Review

**A completed series in Kindle Unlimited.**

**Available in audio, e-book & paperback!**

## THE MYSTIC COVE SERIES

**Wild Irish Heart**

**Wild Irish Eyes**

**Wild Irish Soul**

**Wild Irish Rebel**

**Wild Irish Roots: Margaret & Sean**

**Wild Irish Witch**

**Wild Irish Grace**

**Wild Irish Dreamer**

**Wild Irish Christmas (Novella)**

**Wild Irish Sage**

**Wild Irish Renegade**

**Wild Irish Moon**

———

"I have read thousands of books and a fair percentage have been romances. Until I read Wild Irish Heart, I never had a book actually make me believe in love."- Amazon Review

**A completed series in Kindle Unlimited.**

**Available in audio, e-book & paperback!**

## STAND ALONE NOVELS

### Ms. Bitch

"Ms. Bitch is sunshine in a book! An uplifting story of fighting your way through heartbreak and making your own version of happily-ever-after."

~Ann Charles, USA Today Bestselling Author

### Starting Over Scottish

Grumpy. Meet Sunshine.

She's American. He's Scottish. She's looking for a fresh start. He's returning to rediscover his roots.

### One Way Ticket

A funny and captivating beach read where booking a one-way ticket to paradise means starting over, letting go, and taking a chance on love…one more time

10 out of 10 - The BookLife Prize

# CONTACT ME

I hope my books have added a little magick into your life. If you have a moment to add some to my day, you can help by telling your friends and leaving a review. Word-of-mouth is the most powerful way to share my stories. Thank you.

Love books? What about fun giveaways? Nope? Okay, can I entice you with underwater photos and cute dogs? Let's stay friends, receive my emails and contact me by signing up at my website

As a fun little bonus if you join my newsletter you can celebrate Christmas all year round with a trip back to Grace's Cove. As a welcome gift, I will send you a digital copy of Wild Irish Christmas right to your inbox. Use the link or scan the QR code to get your copy today.

https://offer.triciaomalley.com/free

www.triciaomalley.com

Or find me on Facebook and Instagram.
@triciaomalleyauthor

Made in the USA
Middletown, DE
20 January 2024